THE SHACK

> Grace + Dan
> With my love
> Grandma Anne

THE SHACK

JEANETTE VOYZEY

Sometimes you will never know the value of a moment until it becomes a memory.
(Dr Seuss. 1904 to 1991)

Copyright © 2015 by Jeanette Voyzey.

ISBN:　　　Softcover　　　　978-1-4990-9624-8
　　　　　　eBook　　　　　　978-1-4990-9625-5

All rights reserved. No part of this book may be reproduced or transmitted in any form or by any means, electronic or mechanical, including photocopying, recording, or by any information storage and retrieval system, without permission in writing from the copyright owner.

This is a work of fiction. Names, characters, places and incidents either are the product of the author's imagination or are used fictitiously, and any resemblance to any actual persons, living or dead, events, or locales is entirely coincidental.

Any people depicted in stock imagery provided by Thinkstock are models, and such images are being used for illustrative purposes only.
Certain stock imagery © Thinkstock.

Print information available on the last page.

Rev. date: 03/30/2015

To order additional copies of this book, contact:
Xlibris
800-056-3182
www.Xlibrispublishing.co.uk
Orders@Xlibrispublishing.co.uk
705608

I would like to dedicate my first novel to my three grandchildren, Daniel, Amy and Isabella.

PREFACE

How to make the best of the hand we are dealt? Where do we start? Family and friends maybe, or in Carrie and Charlie's case, meeting the right person, making what at the time seemed to be the right choice, and in some cases, the only option available.

There are always going to be those who criticise, sadly, or those who battle to make some sense of the world around them. How do we cope with the stresses and strains of normal life? I feel the answer is a more simplistic view and would hope to portray this in the following story. I learned a lot from my imaginary family, and although maybe on the surface the tale may seem sugar-coated, the underlying ethos is recognising who you are and being true to yourself.

There are times when life throws a curved ball, just throw it right back . . .

CHAPTER ONE
Jack

'It was the way things were in my family.' This was what Carrie said when I questioned why she, my father, and all relations (well, those that were left) were known by their Christian names rather than Aunt, Uncle, or Mum and Dad.

Carrie (my mother) was an outgoing, lively, and, some would say, pretty woman with a penchant for the finer things in life. Charlie (my father) (whom Carrie insisted on calling Charles even though he once said he was christened Charlie) was the complete opposite. Down to earth, a beer-swilling, cigarette-smoking, hard working, loving father. He idolised Carrie who could do no wrong in his eyes. Carrie, on the other hand, tolerated Charlie in the way a mother tolerated a wayward teenage son. His job was in a factory on the packing floor supervising the running of the conveyor belt which brought us chutneys, pickles, and sauces. You wouldn't have to ask what he did for a living, his aroma would tell you.

I had one sister Phoebe (Carrie chose the name apparently) and a brother Theo (a name which was eventually agreed upon instead of Theodore).

I was the youngest, then Phebes as I call her, and then Theo. Oh, by the way, my name is Jack.

Carrie loved swanning around in a cloud of perfume, furniture polish, and washing-up liquid. Phoebe, small and very dark, had an earthy quality about her which seemed to me a good mix of Carrie and Charlie. Theo well, what was to say about Theo? Tall, blond, handsome, and intelligent and away at university studying something I couldn't even pronounce.

The year was 1976, a long hot summer. Theo was twenty-one, Phebes eighteen, and here I was, a late arrival at twelve.

I never really gave much thought to Carrie and Charlie's ages. I supposed it didn't enter my head. I just felt our life was always going to be one big happy and loving time.

Phoebe was somewhat lost with Theo away because her one game which seemed to occupy her from morning till night was playing him and me off against each other. Being the middle child with two brothers somehow amused her. Very theatrical was Phebes. She hadn't turned any of her A levels into anything I would call useful. Music and dance were her forte. She managed to secure a job at the local college teaching drama and dance with nothing but her enthusiasm and inherent talent to her name. Some people could bluff their way through life, and Phoebe was one of them.

So this was my family, whom I love very much. I looked forward to summer in the shack with Carrie and Charlie and any friends I could bring.

I didn't know the full history of our rustic holiday home. Charlie spoke with some embarrassment of how we acquired this wooden thing on the East Coast of England facing the North Sea. I didn't care. To me, it spelt seaside, rock pools, fish and chips, and not having to wash if I could get away with it!

Phebes declined these days, preferring to spend her time with friends, which Carrie said was fine as she had probably outgrown holidaying with parents. I sensed a slight tremor in Carrie's voice as she said, 'Of course, you don't have to come, darling. I understand.' However, understanding was extremely low on her list. I knew and could tell.

'Right, come on then.' That was Charlie and me. 'Off we go.' How many times had Carrie said this to us all?

What a sight we must look! Tidy wasn't a word that would describe us. Everything was thrown in to our rusty old banger with a cheerfulness not known to the more orderly of our neighbours.

I should say we lived amongst some very influential people, *but*, and it was a big *but*, we had a council house which we rented, whereas most of the other homes around us were bought and owned. Carrie kept our home spic and span; however, her organisational skills when it came to packing left a lot to be desired.

Charlie's wages didn't give us a lot, but we survived in a haze of laughter and love. How on earth we became popular in our community was one question I didn't have an answer to! Everyone really liked us. Carrie had an air of graciousness about her, which appealed to the more discerning of our neighbours. Not least of all, the men who flirted unashamedly in front of their wives, girlfriends, and family, it was considered normal and not offensive in any way. Of course, Carrie lapped it up with delight. Charlie just appeared resigned to it all, just proud to know she was his and joined in the fun and banter. And after all, they did have a son at university even if he had got a grant and a job to pay his way. We had a neighbour called Pat who cared for us when we were younger and still does. She was very much part of our family.

It was the era of the dinner party, so if they found someone willing to put up with me for a few hours and not much money, off they would go to supper, walking home slightly the worse for wear, giggling like a pair of teenagers. When Carrie entertained, we had the best china and her ability to turn the cheapest food into a feast, and me to keep their friends happy with various quips and comments about our laid-back and interesting lifestyle. Because of Charlie's job, we always had interesting sauces on the table. Carrie's stock answer to anyone who asked if they were home-made was always, 'If you look in the rubbish bin, no, but if you don't, yes.' This always produced forced laughter amongst our guests.

Pat, who was our next-door neighbour, was our very best friend.

'Jack, come on, love, before Charles changes his mind,' Carrie said in frustration. Toe-tapping with impatience, Charlie was already losing the will to live knowing he would have to drop us off at the shack and return for work, joining us at the weekend. Just one friend to collect, Freddie. 'Please, Carrie, do not call him Frederick!' Our uninhibited lifestyle didn't appeal to Freddie's parents; however, the thought of losing the responsibility of their offspring for a few days was a deciding factor as I would explain later. Unfortunately, for Carrie, she didn't have that luxury, when not slumming it (as they called it) with us. My pals holidayed abroad which didn't include any of my family. Air fares were out of our reach financially.

We reached the vast expanse of shingle, shale, sand dunes, and weeds that occupied the area around the shack. Having unlocked the door and thrown anything not needed outside, including the deck chairs, Carrie lit the Calor gas burner to make tea, before Charlie left again.

I waved Charlie off with a hint of sadness. His three-week holiday allowance a year didn't give him much time, so he did what a lot of others in a similar situation did: he booked long weekends. 'Bye, Charlie, see you soon,' I shouted above the sound of wheels on gravel and a north-easterly breeze.

We knew he secretly liked the time to himself. He could watch our antiquated television and drink what he liked, without Carrie to admonish him and tell him to stop being so lazy. Phoebe was around to cook for him, although he was quite capable of doing so for himself. He took it all in good part as he neither indulged too much nor was lazy. We have the best garden in the street, all his handiwork and some of Theo's. All three of us were home tutored by Carrie, which we all enjoyed very much, well most of the time anyway.

So now began the best summer of my life. I write about this one because although there were others, this was the one I enjoyed the most. The weather was glorious. The sea although calm had an angry greyness about it which didn't encourage swimming. This was just as well, because some years ago, Theo was caught in a rip tide and only survived because he was a very strong swimmer. He had defied the 'No Swimming Allowed' notices and his parents' warning and took off at speed to the nearest tethered buoy. He was picked up by a passing trawler man, who didn't stop calling Theo unprintable names, and even after practically throwing him out in the safety of the shallows, his voice still carried on the air long after Carrie and Charlie had finished their rant too. They very rarely raised their voices to any of us. This was out of fear thinking they may lose their son.

'Right, off you both go,' Carrie said. Tea (which I knew would be something like scrambled eggs) was sometime around five. 'Come on, Freddie, there is someone I want you to meet,' I said as I grabbed him by the arm. We ran as fast as our legs could carry us to the fishermen's hut to check if Albert was there mending his nets, to beg again for the chance to go fishing with him. 'Oh, not you, two varmints!' he shouted. 'I thought I'd seen the last of u' um.' Albert hadn't noticed I had brought Freddie this time and not Joseph who normally came with us. 'You lot in that shed again?' 'Lucky for u'um, Ned don't need it any more since e be dead and got no family. Don't come 'ere mithering me else a clip around the ear will come yur way.' We knew Albert was joking. He got up and gave us a bear hug which almost knocked the stuffing out of us. Albert was anything but small. His eyes were the colour of a summer sky; reflected in them was a kindness and sometimes weariness after long hours at sea, hauling in huge nets of mainly mackerel and the odd rogue cod if he was lucky. His eyebrows were a grey bushy forest, in competition with his beard which was a strange shade of the same grey and a browny colour caused by the pipe which never seemed to be out of his mouth. I loved the smell, a mixture of pipe smoke and oil cloth which surrounded him. During the winter months, he ran a market stall in the local town square selling anything he could get his hands on to make a living, junk it looked like to me, but Carrie said, 'Beauty is in the eye of the beholder,' when I asked how he ever managed to sell anything. Holiday makers were thin on the ground in this part of the world, so most of his catch went to the local fishmonger who was more than happy to pay a fair price.

'Is that your hose attached to the tap?' I asked. 'What's it to u'um, lad?' 'Well, our water container is almost empty, and we will need to fill it later.' We knew the fishermen used the water to hose down the decks when they returned and unloaded their catch.

We always had a problem turning on the tap mainly because men like Albert with their strong grip turned it so tightly it almost came off the wall.

I once asked a miserable-looking man who just happened to be wandering by if he knew who owned the tap and water and found out after a brief history lesson that it was fitted by the owners of a house which once stood behind the wall. I was too short to peer over, but I could see the house no longer existed.

'I'll get rid o' the 'ose lads soes you can have yur water just as soon as I finish wi me boat and net.'

'Thanks, Albert. See you tomorrow.'

'Not if I sees e first,' he shouted followed by a throaty chuckle.

Freddie and I wandered back to the shack just in time to see Carrie walking back from the opposite direction trying to fend off a dog which seemed to think he had found a new friend. Carrie liked dogs. When I asked if we could have one, the answer was always no. 'I struggle to feed us lot, so any animal is out of the question' was always her answer. 'Besides which I have enough to cope with, teaching you which has never been easy.'

'Thanks, Carrie.'

'You are welcome.' She laughed.

Freddie said being with us was an education, and he loved the freedom. I had come to know him so much better since our first meeting in our local park one afternoon in early February. Carrie, Charlie, and I were out on what they called a constitutional, that's a walk to you and me! Freddie was walking towards us kicking stones and anything he could find. We all said hello in passing, and Freddie stopped to talk. He was bordering on tears which I found hard to take in. He was a big lad but no older than me. It transpired he was under enormous pressure from his parents to do well at school. Because we were homeschooled by Carrie and often told, 'All I want for my children is for them to be happy and healthy,' the idea of a pushy parent sounded horrendous. We exchanged names and addresses, and

Carrie said she was more than happy to help him regarding his school work with his parents' permission.

Apparently, his mother was horrified at the thought. Freddie told me she thought we were nothing more than gypsies with our rust bucket of a car, always loaded with mattresses, blankets, etc. For a while, we heard no more from him. Embarrassment probably kept him away. However, his father's 'highly paid and highly stressful job' claimed a victim when he had a heart attack. Freddie came to see us saying his mother was hysterical even though his dad's prognosis was good (being youngish and relatively strong, he would survive) 'Mum can't take it in,' he said. 'She says she is sorry for the things she said, and can I please spend time here as Jack is my only friend outside school who is living close to us?' Not too close though and not part of Carrie and Charlie's group. His peers were either abroad on holiday or trying to outdo each other with talk of future destinations. We are hardly what you would call friends, but we said okay, because in a way, I liked him and knew I could draw out of him more than what it seemed was on the surface.

Freddie's mum, Janice or Jackie or something like it, said he could come to the shack, more out of exasperation than anything. She knew caring for her husband (I think she said Neil) was going to be a full-time job until he was well enough to work again. Snobbery didn't rule that household any more! However, Carrie had more class in her little finger than all of them put together.

That was how Freddie came to be with us. He laughed and ran and enjoyed our impromptu beach barbecues. Oh yes, I forgot to say we brought our old metal barrel with the grill across the top. Our lifestyle was alien to him, but he sucked it in and fed on it like a hungry animal.

I saw my privileged life through Freddie's eyes and not for the first time counted my lucky stars.

Now for more fun. Albert kept his word and took the hose off the tap. Carrie boiled water for our 'swill down'. 'Look the other way, please, boys,' she pleaded. So we did whilst she washed and put on her nightwear. We just took our water outside and laughed and soaked each other whilst Carrie made cocoa. It was a still warm night, and there was light enough to watch the small fishing boats make their way out to sea, even though it was coming up to nine o'clock at night. We filled the water carrier again for the morning and sat on the veranda drinking our hot cocoa, eating biscuits, and planning the next day. Freddie was amused by Carrie's china cups and saucers. 'We had mugs,' he said. Like I mentioned before, Carrie had a style. Our supper of scrambled eggs and crusty bread had been served on bone china plates. Our fruits were stored in a crystal bowl on the rickety shelf.

The thin spongy mattresses on our bunks were not too comfortable, but we were so tired by nightfall we didn't notice. 'No arguments, Freddie, the top bunk is mine,' I said as I hunted for my torch to read a comic. 'You're okay, Jack,' he replied, 'I don't like heights.'

We disappeared under our blankets to block out the beam from the distant lighthouse and listened to the sound of the sea. The nights in the shack were very special, so it wasn't the South of France or Marbella, but hey, it was us – the Connaught/Jones family – and I knew I would remember these times for the rest of my life.

Carrie had finished her history lesson which I heard during every visit. She was proud of her knowledge and spent time researching the marshlands in great depth, but this time it was for Freddie's benefit.

There was Prospect House owned by the director and writer Derek Jarman, with black clapperboard with yellow paintwork and the poem 'The Sun Rising' by John Donne etched in the timbers. Derek was famous for his garden as well as his journalistic prowess. His Caravaggio work was of particular interest to Carrie as her forte was Art History along with her degree in Mathematics. The Nuclear Power Station Commissioned in 1960 hadn't materialised, but plans were still in place to build and activate it.

The church on Romney Marsh dedicated to Thomas a Becket serving the village of Fairfield which has long since disappeared. The village, that is, the church still stood. Carrie knew it all. A mine of information passed on to our enquiring minds.

CHAPTER TWO
Jack

My information and the telling of the next part of this story came from the journals Carrie wrote during her lifetime. I found these amongst her possessions when we cleared the house. Both Phebes and Theo took copies.

I didn't really know much about Theo's thoughts regarding the *the shack*. There were a few references later, but nothing to say how he really felt. He was with our parents on a nature walk on the muddy bleak marshland when they came across the abandoned hut. An old fishing net hung from the roof, left to dry, timbers missing, and altogether a wreck. There were just miles of emptiness with the exception of a long abandoned rowing boat rotting away near the water's edge. 'Well,' said Charlie, 'not much sign of life here.' That was the beginning of our acquisition of what was to become our holiday home.

Charlie said he would come at weekends and work on the shack and if any one questioned what he was doing, he would plead ignorance (he was good at that) and give up. Week by week he came back saying no one had said a word to him. He was greeted on the odd occasion by beachcombers with some contraption (as he called it) looking for treasure. It was 1962. Theo was seven years old and already showing signs of brilliance; Phoebe was three and a real show-off, entertaining anyone who would watch and listen. How do I know this? Carrie never stopped reminiscing about her wonderful children as she called them.

CHAPTER THREE
Carrie

Here we were on windswept Dungeness. 'Why do I feel so stupidly happy?' Carrie wrote. I supposed I felt I had it all. Charles, Theo, and Phoebe all together. I never had or wanted much, just my family and a few prized possessions left to me by my parents, mainly china and a beautiful marquetry tray which I used to serve whatever beverage was favourite at the time. These amazingly survived the blitz which destroyed our home.

I watched my children building what I thought was a sandcastle. (Theo was happy now – he was engaged in something constructive.) It was more grey clay than sand, but the mix was good at sticking together without too much water which would have turned it in to a soggy mess. 'That's great,' I shout to them over the wind. 'Will there be a princess living in your castle?' 'Oh, for goodness sake, Carrie!' Theo's voice had an air of superiority which belied his years. 'Its an house for crabs.' I laughed saying, 'It's "a house, Theo." That's what I just said,' exasperation now written all over his face. He wandered off looking for guests for his newly built house. 'Please look after Phoebe,' I called. They went off hand in hand in search of crabs, a bucket swinging from his free hand.

As I watched my children wandered off, I started to think back, not for the first time how I came to be here.

I am Caroline Connaught. All of my friends call me Carrie, well, friends and just about everyone else.

The sun was beating down on my uncovered head as I scanned the local paper for work. I had graduated from Oxford with a first in

Mathematics and Art History. It was 1952, and we were surrounded by post-war gloom. I didn't mind what I did. I just needed something to take the edge off the loneliness and frustration at not being able to join in with the friends (whom I shared a house with) through lack of funds. I had survived on the little money left to me by my parents. They were killed during the war when an ambulance on its way to an emergency (one of many) had crashed into their Morris Austin with such force they hadn't stood a chance. It was 1942, and I was just twelve years old. They were on their way to a village just outside Oxford to collect me from an ageing great-aunt called Maude.

'Could you budge up please?' I looked up blinking in the sunshine, and there he was, the man of my dreams. I had a thing for the film star Tony Curtis, and this Adonis looking down at me was a very good replica. I blushed pink and then scarlet and then developed a stutter which I hadn't noticed before. Neither had I noticed that the fine weather had brought out most of Oxford and they were all sat in this pub garden. I had sprawled across the bench with bag on one end and books on the other with my newspaper and me taking up the rest of it. My half a pint of lager was now warm and flat. I wasn't sure if I could drink it any way, my throat had closed over. In my rush to pick everything up, my drink went flying all over me, paper and bench. Mr Adonis laughed and said, 'Hey, I didn't mean to cause this mayhem. I just wanted a seat. Stay there. I will get you another lager. Is that what you drink, or is there something else?' I wanted to say a stiff brandy but thought better of it.

'Charlie Jones is the name. What's yours?'
'Cccccarolyn Connaught,' I stuttered. 'Plllleased to meet you.'
'Well, Miss Connaught, no wedding ring I see. It must be my lucky day! What brings you here this bright sunny afternoon?' Do I tell him that my housemates were in the South of France on holiday and I couldn't afford to go or do I just say I fancied some fresh air, and you, if you are up for it.

'I settled for the fresh air. And what brings you here? I detect a slight Welsh accent.'

'River dredging, that's the job. Sorry not a brain surgeon or a scientist.' The way I felt he could be a road sweeper or public toilet cleaner for all I cared. 'Well, we have a few rivers around here to keep you occupied, The Cherwell, The Thames, The Windrush . . . Well, I am working somewhere not far from here called Port Meadow whichever one that is. It's not very deep. Just needed a good clean out. I understand it's popular with swimmers?' 'Probably,' said Carrie, 'if you don't mind the floating cow pats!'

I downed my lager in one, more because I was thirsty and I didn't want to spill this one.

We chatted for an hour or so before we decided to walk back to my digs. I explained I needed a job and would probably end up on the streets if I didn't get a move on. 'Well, Miss Connaught.' Ever the gentleman Charlie shook my hand. 'Very nice to meet you. I'm off to meet some mates for a game of darts. Can I see you again?' I wanted to shout, 'Yes, please,' at the top of my voice, but I tried to play hard to get against my better judgement. 'Oh, come on, Carrie, yes or no?' I was shaken by the Carrie bit and just nodded. 'Righto, see you tomorrow in the pub 7.30 ish.' My hands shook as I tried to unlock the front door. He must have girls queuing around the corner. Why on earth would he bother with me? Maybe he even had a wife tucked away in deepest Wales.

Even though I sat in the bar the next evening, I really didn't expect Charles to appear, but there he was larger than life and twice as handsome. 'So, lager is it?' my lovely Charles asked. 'Well, I might go mad and have a pint of beer if that's okay. Have what you like, Carrie. It's Friday and pay day.' 'Thank you, Charles,' I spluttered. 'My name is Charlie. That's the name my parents gave me.'

'I prefer Charles,' I said rather tentatively.

'Okay, Charles it is, but don't expect me to answer to it.'

'Okay, Charles!'

'Right, walkies,' Charles said an hour later. 'Come and see how much I have done today.' We walked across Port Meadow. Piled high above the bank was the silt dredged from the river. 'How much longer are you here for?' I asked.

'Probably a week or two. Then off to some other bunged up river bed somewhere.'

Blue eyes jet-black hair, me a mousey blonde and green eyes, the colour of a tabby cats, what fascinating babies we would have. I blushed at the thought.

'So, Miss Connaught, tell me about yourself.' Charles was inquisitive and wanted to delve into my life. Does that mean he was single and unattached? Could be, dare I ask? 'No, you first,' I said. This was one way of finding out. 'Not much to tell.' His laughter rang in the air. 'Twenty-three years old, single, live in a bedsit in Llanelli, did have a cat called Christopher till he got run over.' I practically choked on my own saliva.

'Why would you call a cat Christopher?'

'Why not?' he said. 'Just wanted something other than Smudge. Blackie or Tabby.' Fair enough, I suppose.

'Now your turn.'

'Okay,' I say with trepidation. 'Orphaned during the war, brought up by my aunt Maude, won a place at university, just graduated from Oxford with a first in Maths and Art History. No pets, no money, and no job.'

'Wow, you have the brains though, well done you! Beauty and brains a great combination,' Charles said as he turned to look at me directly in the eye.

I found it really hard to read and understand Carrie's notes. Her story jumped a bit from the shack to meeting Charlie and back to the shack, but I supposed that was how her mind worked at the time – trying to encompass everything that was happening to her. I carried on reading and wondered how she felt putting everything into words.

The sound of Theo and Phoebe's laughter as they came back with the bucket swinging between them brought me back to the present with a jolt.

Theo lined up his house guests, but they were not so keen to take up residence. They walked sideways away from the entrance to this hastily constructed mud home. Phoebe had lost interest since one particular crab had grabbed her finger and made it bleed. I had bathed it and wrapped it and made what we called a dolly of her little finger. Charles had cuddled her until she stopped crying. I had filled hot water bottles to put in their bunks and called them in for their nightly swill down. Charles had gone for a shallow swim. Theo had his torch and would read a story for Phoebe. Charles and I had a bottle of wine to drink on the wooden plateau in front of the shack. Yes, I know I called him Charles, but this was my journal. Everyone else called him Charlie. Theo said he thought the crabs were extremely ungrateful not to like their new home and he would be having stern words with them in the morning. I didn't like to tell him they would be gone by then and would probably be in a fisherman's net.

It was as I thought, the next morning. Neither Theo's collection of crabs nor their home were to be seen anywhere. 'Well, I am eight tomorrow, and when I am nine, I won't come back here again,' Theo announced. 'Oh right,' I said, 'where are you planning to go.'

'I haven't decided yet, I will let you know.' Precocious sprang to mind, but somehow I cannot attach that label to my son. I loved him so much. He takes after my father whom I adored. Tall for his age with the same hair colour as mine, now bleached by the sun, and his tanned limbs all too long for an eight-year-old. He was going to be tall. Phoebe, whom I loved equally, was much more compliant, so much younger, of course. Small and dark like my mother and very much the colouring of Charles, black hair and blue eyes with a soft trusting nature. Charles adored both his children; however, he was so gentle with Phoebe. She was aware she could wrap him around her little finger (the one that wasn't bitten by the crab).

Losing both my parents had left part of me still very raw. It seemed like only yesterday I had the sad news.

Maude's front door bell shattered the silence of her living room. We were both reading, waiting for my parents. 'Here they are,' Maude said in her dreary tone.

Two police officers greeted her when she opened the door. 'Miss Transem?' they asked. 'Can we come in?' They didn't wait for an answer. 'Please sit down. We have grave news.' So began my time with Maude. First of all, she was kindness itself. Then I was told in no uncertain terms I needed an education and would have to support myself as we had no family left. She decided I was going to be the very best at anything I tried.

How did I cope? Well, I really don't know. I would never have believed that when I said goodbye to my parents Carole and John, I would never see them again. After the funerals and the 'I am so sorry for your loss dear' from various people I had never seen before, I tried to put my life back together again. I had no choice but to stay with Maude. My parents rented their home, and it was destroyed by a doodlebug anyway. We lived too close to the industrial part of Oxford to be safe. School was not my favourite place. I tried to learn as best I could, but somehow my mind wouldn't function. Maude got more and more frustrated with me, and being an ex-teacher, she decided home tutoring was the way to go. A visit from the headmaster didn't go too well either. He made it very clear that if she took me out of school, there was no going back. Maude was very pedantic about everything, not in the least bit flexible. I either learned or I didn't. Sitting there every morning in her tweed skirt, woolly jumper, and brogues, she was a formidable sight and instilled a mixture of fright and awe in me. My friends were welcome as long as they had good manners. 'Yes, Miss Transem. No, Miss Transem. Three bags full, Miss Transem,' we muttered behind her back.

My mind was a jumble of memories which overtake the present sometimes. Losing my parents, my time at university, and then meeting Charles had all merged in to one blurred image.

So Charles announced as we walked hand in hand along the Cherwell, 'I think I might love you, Miss Caroline Connaught.' I didn't know whether to laugh or cry. He was coming to the end of his river-dredging duties in Oxfordshire. Next stop Kent. 'Don't suppose you would fancy sharing a grotty room in a not particularly salubrious area with an itinerant river cleaner? No probably not. You have a brain in your head, mine is in a bucket.' I laughed and cried in equal measure. I might be an Oxford graduate, but apart from a bit of teaching and work in a bar in the evenings, there was nothing to keep me here. I thought of becoming an eternal student and doing a postgraduate course, but money wouldn't allow and besides which I might have a degree, a first at that, but I don't think my overdeveloped mind could take any more.

Maude had long since gone to teach grannies to suck eggs in heaven. Sorry, I shouldn't be so rude. She cared for me when I had no one else and orchestrated my journey in to university. I think she tolerated me rather than loved me. However, we managed together to turn a devastating happening in to a manageable life.

'Are you listening, Carrie?' Charles spoke with a frustration I hadn't heard before. 'So sorry, I am just surprised that's all.'

'Well, you went off in trance and were heading for a coma. Am I that boring?' I didn't like to tell him I was considering what to do and reminiscing about Maude and her strict ways blurred with the horror of losing my parents.

Charles knew about Carole and John and still to this day, how vulnerable I felt. His voice softened slightly and he whispered, 'Well?'

I wanted to shout, 'You bet I will come with you,' but I still couldn't believe this gorgeous man said he loved me. Me with the mousy blonde hair, although two shades lighter from the late summer/autumn sun and eyes the colour of a tabby cats. 'What's to lose?' came tumbling out of my mouth before I had a chance to think. 'Oh thanks,' Charles said feigning hurt, clutching his chest where his heart is. 'I am so sorry. It's just I don't want to get hurt, and I cannot believe this is happening to me.'

'Apart from the fact that you call me Charles which deserves a punch on the nose, there is no way I would ever hurt you, Carrie! I fell in love with you the moment I asked you to budge up on the pub garden bench.' 'Ditto,' I said, although I didn't add, my feelings were more lust than love at the time.

CHAPTER FOUR
Jack

The holidays in the shack were greeted with hilarity by everyone, except me, of course. I wasn't even a twinkle as they say at the beginning of their time in remote isolation. Charlie had decked the front with balloons and streamers which blew in the north-easterly wind and looked liked colourful sweeties and ribbons against the brown paint and the grey skies. Carrie wrote, 'The shack was unrecognisable.' Charlie had built a wooden platform at the front and two wooden steps. We had a smart door painted sea green with brass hinges holding it in place. A lock and two bolts completed the picture. It was half-term and cold. Carrie brought hot water bottles, soup, and blankets. 'We couldn't believe our luck,' Carrie wrote. I said I didn't know much about Theo's thoughts. Seeing him now, I would think he was slightly embarrassed by it all. His head was always stuck in a book, or he was asking questions which baffled Charlie but pleased Carrie. Her firstborn was going to be quite brilliant!

Theo sat on the beach with his oversized red jumper on, not for the first time asking, 'What on earth are we doing here?' He seemed bored to death with the whole experience. Phebes was sitting with him and laughing and seemingly oblivious to the cold wind whistling around their ears. 'Come on, you two,' Charlie shouted. 'Let's play cricket.' This outdoorsy thing was not appealing to Theo. Carrie wrote about her son in such glowing terms. Charlie just said, 'Cheer up, or else, next time, you are home alone.' 'So what?' said Theo, apparently. Charles loved his son, but didn't understand him. Communication was difficult because Theo was exasperated with nearly everything Charles said, and 'some of what I had to say come to that,' Carrie wrote.

The cricket match was very one-sided, just Phebes and Charlie chasing a ball with a bat that had seen better days. Carrie made hot chocolate for Theo saying, 'There, there,' patting his head, which I would think irritated the life out of him.

Carrie related we had walked for what seemed like miles across the empty landscape broken up by the odd abandoned fishing hut, boats, and nets, collecting driftwood to dry for our ancient barrel barbecue. If we were lucky, there was some coal as well. Phoebe collected shells and some very odd-looking skeletal bits washed a bright white by the tide. Were they once a bird, a fish, who knows? Theo decided things were not quite so bad after all. He was friends with Albert, our local fisherman, who although quite dismissive of our presence at first, always asked if he wanted to go fishing. 'I'll be in the shallows misses e won't come to any 'arm I bin fishin these wa'ers for some yers. I noes when things are calm and when they ain't.' 'I reluctantly let him go but not Phoebe,' she protested for a while. She then said, 'I don't want to go any way I might get eaten by sharks!' 'I got spare life jacket, missus, and so 'wester so don't u'um fret if yur wants we can get some mackerel fur yurs tea.'

We always invited Albert to share our supper. He caught, gutted, and cleaned it so it only seemed polite. 'U' um got any soap, misses, soes I can wash me 'ands.'

'Help yourself, Albert,' I said, handing him what was left of our bar of Lifebuoy. We all grew to love him. He was our one connection with the world outside of our friends and family. There was a Mrs Albert, but we never met her. We sometimes wondered if she was a figment of his imagination.

As we sat after supper watching the tide receding and the stars appearing, I started reminiscing again following the road that brought us here.

CHAPTER FIVE

Carrie

Charles went back to Wales to collect his Kent job sheets and instructions, also his few possessions. This was going to be a long assignment – beach dredging this time. I packed up my troubles in my old kit bag as the song goes. Very near the mark for me, I didn't own a suitcase, so it was an old bag. The rest of the song says, 'Smile, smile, smile.' Well, I had a grin on my face the size of a Cheshire cat. My friends and flatmates said they would exchange all their time in St Tropez for one night with Charlie. 'Get lost,' I jested, 'I saw him first.' We hugged and kissed goodbye, and I promised to keep in touch. 'Phew yes when you come up for air,' they giggled.

'Beep beep,' the sound of the horn summoned me outside followed by my three friends, all anxious for one last look at Charles. Smiling and charm itself, Charles got out of his car, which looked as if it was held together by luck and paint, and gave each one a hug, five minutes of blushes and laughing, and we were off. 'Bye, see you soon,' I shouted. My last look (for now) at the dreaming spires, my memories, were coming with me. All this may seem ad hoc to readers, but it paved the way for our life together. We lived on a wing and a prayer, it was how we were. Although opposites in many ways, we had the same ideas about our final destination. Children, yes, definitely, but not just yet. Marriage, um, not sure on that one. Every moment with Charles was magic. We would probably live hand to mouth for the rest of our lives. I made up my mind when we settled in Kent that I would make use of my degree, either by home tutorials or in a gallery.

It was in a museum in the end, grand title of curator, salary less than grand, but it paid the bills. Ship wrecks, press gangs, stories of piracy, keelhauling, it was all there. I learnt very quickly and became adept at explaining all to the many visitors who were hungry for information about the exhibitions they were viewing. It saved them reading the blurb so beautifully printed and artistically designed by my goodself but somehow wasted on most.

I organised cheese and wine evenings to attract sponsors and flirted and cajoled money from the richer businesses in the area. I organised school tea parties, fancy dress (come as a pirate), and all in all lifted the museum's profile in the space of a year.

If Charles said, 'Ahoy me hearties,' once more when I arrived home, I would strangle him. How things have changed, when we first met it was Tony Bennett's 'Because of you'. He can't sing for toffee, but at least, the latter was tolerable! 'Way-hay and up she rises.' 'Shut up, Charles, if you want to see your next birthday.' Our life was far from perfect, nothing ever was, but we loved being together. Our cramped accommodation organised by Charles's firm was anything but comfortable, but beggars can't be choosers.

Charles enjoyed his work. How on earth he did I don't understand. Shifting masses of silt and gravel everyday from one place to another wasn't exactly fun. He said he managed before he met me spending time in the pubs in the locality in which he was working, meeting locals, and playing darts. His diet left a lot to be desired too, fish and chips. 'It came wrapped in newspaper and tasted good,' he said. 'Really?' I said, 'Not every day, surely?' 'No, I can cook you know! Just didn't have the facilities sometimes.'

After eighteen months of hard graft and lots of tears and laughter peppered with the odd argument, really childish ones, 'You are so stupid!' 'No, I am not, you are,' our voices reverberating around our bedsit, I woke one morning feeling yuck. I had been exhausted for a couple of months and no periods. I had an appointment to see the doctor. I thought I was anaemic and overworked. I couldn't be pregnant surely. Charles and I were so careful. Then I remembered the night we had been out with some newly acquired friends. The women in the group flirted outrageously with Charles, so I got more than a little tipsy and let them get on with it.

We arrived home shortly after midnight. 'Come here, you gorgeous creature,' Charles shouted. The rest as they say was history. So up the duff that was me. No children allowed where we lived, so I had to leave work, and also we would be homeless. Fortunately, in the end, job-wise I was okay. I had enough volunteers who said, 'Bring him or her in, and we will help as much as we can.'

Our communal bathroom at home, although kept clean by the overly large lady who sang mostly out of tune and irritatingly loud for the duration of her time mopping the kitchen, bathroom, and hallway, we had one tenant who used a very strong perfume, and even though some mornings I didn't feel sick, one whiff of her scent was enough to induce spasms of retching for at least half an hour. We had used the outdoor salt water swimming pool down by the seafront a lot, and now, we just took our washing kit with us for afterwards. Instead of just a quick dip in and out of the showers, we luxuriated in them spreading foam everywhere.

My bump grew, and I grew angry at the choice of maternity wear. Flipping heck! Who wanted to look like Doris Day with a big white bow at my neck supposedly to draw the eye away from the stomach! Well, the pleats down the front really gave the game away. Sorry, Doris, this isn't personal. It just isn't my choice. I readjusted my clothes to fit. They mainly had small waists and big skirts, lots of material to play with. I was about as familiar with a needle and thread as George Washington was to lies! Somehow though I made use of the yards of surplus material.

Fortunately, I didn't grow to a gargantuan size and managed quite well. Charles's favourite saying, 'You cannot wear that,' fell on deaf ears. Besides which my polite staff always said, 'You look nice, Carrie,' never, 'You look wonderful' or ' you are glowing'. In the scheme of things, nice will do nicely, thank you.

Everything was going well in the museum. Mr 'I Can Do Anything You Want, Just Ask' was busy trying to fit a square peg in a round hole quite literally, building a replica of a wreck supposed to lie in the ocean just of Folkeston harbour. Then, oh help, a wet floor around my chair! I wasn't due for three weeks, but I knew enough from my visits to the maternity wing of the local hospital that this was it. An image of the nurse/midwife hovered before my eyes. I wasn't in the mood for her today, but very obviously my baby was. If she pursed her thin lips at me and said, 'Not married then, dear,' I won't be responsible for my actions. Nurse Wellington (the old boot) was to be my attendee as she called it. 'You do the work, and I assist.' 'Oh really, is that all there is to it?' I thought, knowing full well it wasn't.

Sheila, my able assistant, offered to drive me to the hospital. At least I won't flood her foot well, that bits already done and watered all over my office floor. Mary was mopping frantically before we opened to the public.

Mr I Can Do . . . offered to go down to the water's edge to tell Charles I was off. He had what was left of our car, parked in the car park reserved for workmen in and around the seafront. My bag packed ready was on the back seat. Very organised for me. But I knew I would have to be, we were on our own. 'Please remind him to bring my bag in,' I told Mary.

'Righto, boss.'

'Oh and by the way, Mary, he is a flirt. Just because you are over fifty, don't think you are immune to his charms. No female is. How do you think I got here?'

'Don't worry, Carrie. I went off all of that years ago,' Mary said with a strangulated laugh.

'So, Mrs Connaught.' 'Miss,' I said through pain and gritted teeth. 'Here we are. Make yourself comfortable, and I will fetch the doctor.' Comfortable! Really, have you tried lying on a narrow bed in a maternity ward, twice the size you normally are and hanging over the sides? I had a flashback then which made me smile and eased my aching stomach. Charles and me in his single bed the first time we made love. We giggled so much we ended up on the floor. My reverie was broken by the appearance of Nurse Wellington and a doctor who looked about sixteen. After a brief examination, I was told to rest and he would be back to see me in an hour or so. 'Your husband is here and in the father's waiting room. If you want to wander along to see him, you turn right out of here and first left. I clutched my stomach as a wave of pain and nausea grabbed me. 'Are you sure I am not ready to give birth?' I asked, along with, 'He is not my husband.' The old boot pursed her lips again. 'I forgot to tell you, Doctor Walker, this one is not married.' 'No, you are not ready,' she said with a sniff, 'it will be awhile yet.' I poked my tongue out at her substantial rear as she went out of the door forgetting I was at her mercy.

I wandered down the corridor in my hospital gown feeling like Billy Bunter. Charles was ensconced in a comfortable armchair with a cup of tea, no doubt brought to him by a tea lady with her trolley who thought all her Christmases had come at once. No woman I knew had ignored Charles, so I didn't think she would be any different. I was right. She popped her head around the door. 'Would you like a biscuit, dear?' She took one look at me and scarpered before he had a chance to answer. I had the feeling Charles was not quite sure what to say. He didn't like the idea of me grunting and doubled up in pain but was also glad he wouldn't have to be around for the gory bit.

CHAPTER SIX
Carrie

Theodore'able came in to the world just two hours after the old boot and the doctor had said I wasn't ready. It was a lively if somewhat quick birth. He weighed in at a respectable 6 lbs 9 ozs. Not too bad for an early baby. Nurse Wellington went to get Charles. 'Mr Jones, you have a son,' she announced with some authority. We had discussed names but always argued over Theodore. Looking at my son with hair the colour of ripe peaches all stuck up on end and the frown across his forehead, he looked like a professor trying to solve the mystery of the universe. I knew at that moment he was going to be very special. Ever the peace maker and joyously happy Charles said he would compromise, our son was to be Theo. 'Well, Mr Jones, you have two weeks to find us somewhere to live.'

'Okay, Miss Connaught, your will is my command.' Nurse Wellington to my surprise had a tear in her eye. 'It always gets me every time,' she said, 'the miracle of life.' I felt sorry for my previous treatment of her and vowed I would never call her an old boot again.

Charles gave me a huge hug and very gently hugged Theo. 'I am so, so proud of you, Carrie. Thank you so much for my beautiful son.' His lovely blue eyes were full of tears as he left us to go home. I knew I had never been happier in the whole of my life. Getting my degree paled in to insignificance to giving birth to my gorgeous son. Taken by surprise at the sudden mix of emotions I felt, I cried myself to sleep, and for the next couple of days, I felt very tearful. 'Don't worry, it is quite normal,' Nurse Wellington informed me. Having got over the mortal sin of us not being married, she somehow became a kind of a friend. I learnt the pursed lips were normal for her owing to some missing teeth and not a sign of distaste. I wished I hadn't judged her so harshly.

After a few days, I perked up when Sheila and Mary visited. Charles had been very well looked after during my absence. They had taken casseroles, pies, and beer to help him survive (poor love). All this female attention was not unfamiliar to him.

Charles was trying hard to find us somewhere to live. 'A couple of streets away, there are some boarded up houses,' he told me. I think they were council. They were to be demolished for a road-widening scheme to accommodate the steady flow of vehicles on to our roads, however, a reprieve, and whilst they were going to lose their front gardens, which are exceptionally long, a green area was to be laid all along the front of the five houses which would be looked after by the council and would be available to remove if the road-widening scheme was reconsidered. 'I have enquired,' he said. 'Because of our situation we can rent one, although the council really wanted to sell them. That was the idea behind removing the gardens. The houses could stay put.' We couldn't afford to buy, so renting it was.'

We brought Theo home in our beat-up old wreck knowing we would have to buy something more reliable to carry our precious cargo and all the paraphernalia that goes with a new baby.

Charles had managed to move our few possessions without breaking a single thing. 'Please look after my china,' I pleaded. 'It was Carole's and she loved it.'

I wasn't too happy when Charles decided he needed to change his job, Theo and I loved watching him work along the seafront. He loved the sound of the dredger. His work here had been extended for one more year and then we could be going anywhere. 'Unless you want to become a nomad,' he said, 'besides we like it here and are settled, I need something more permanent.' He managed to find a work as a supervisor in the local factory producing pickles and things like that. Well, he would, wouldn't he? The interviewer was a lady, albeit middle-aged and quite plain according to Charles? I imagined her simpering and flirting with Charles completely forgetting what she was supposed to be doing.

Our new home was surprisingly large which made our sparse possessions look even more meagre, but it was home and that was all that mattered. Charles had managed to make it look presentable putting Carole's china away out of sight not wanting to tempt fate and break it. I went back to work in the museum with Theo much to everyone's delight. I wasn't going to be parted from my son by anyone or anything. Charles (in spite of sleepless nights) had permanent smile on his face. He enjoyed his new job and earned more money doing overtime whenever it was offered. More than ever, he loved spending time with his son.

We managed quite well and bought a car which had seen better days but was more reliable and had less rust than the last one.

We spent our weekends travelling around getting to know the area and had made a few friends amongst our neighbours.

It was during one of these jaunts we saw the shack. 'You cannot be serious,' I said to Charles when he suggested it as a holiday home. 'Don't worry, Carrie Connaught. I will revive this pile of wood in to something worth having.'

'But how can you? It may belong to someone.'

Charlie smiled and tapped the side of his nose in a knowing way. 'I will spend my weekends here working to rebuild this pile of timbers. If I am questioned, I will just say sorry, didn't realise it belonged to someone. I was just using it as a project!' What project he had in mind was a mystery to me.

I could not believe the miracle Charles wrought on this old shed. He built bunks, shelves, cupboards, and installed a gas burner. We even had a window. The door, I have to say, looked more solid than the rest of it with brass hinges and locks. I thought our new holiday home was in the most desolate place on earth, but somehow, I loved it because Charles had done so much to make it comfortable for us.

Our first holiday in the shack was greeted with some comments from our neighbours, mainly on how we are going to manage when we told them where we were going. Our ancient reliable car was stacked to the roof with blankets, hot water bottles, food, and our barbecue made out of an old oil drum.

Theo was three years old and already very inquisitive about the world around him. We laughed and sang our week away. Nursery rhymes, modern pop songs, usually Elvis. I was surprised Charles did a very good impression even if he couldn't sing.

We read stories to Theo at night, trying to break through and find out what interested him. He wasn't naughty, just somehow remote in his own little world. He enjoyed the rock pools and collected fishy creepy-crawlies as he called the odd things which appeared in his jam jar. We had an old bucket which we filled with water and tipped all his finds in for him to keep, adding seaweed for good measure.

'Oh, it's the shed dwellers,' my neighbour Pat said when we arrived home. I knew she was joking, and to be honest, I didn't really care what people thought. She seemed immune to Charles's charms unlike the rest of the female population. As I write, I think why readers would think I trusted him. Well, as Mrs Wallis Simpson once said when asked how she maintained her looks, 'A woman who is loved is truly beautiful.' I wasn't stunningly pretty. I knew that, but I was told I had a certain unusual look. This came about because I knew I was loved in a Charles Jones's kind of way. Although I had been told on a few occasions I was quite attractive, I really wasn't that bothered. I loved and trusted Charles with my whole being.

I recognised the waves of nausea and my growing body all too soon. I was now pregnant again. Fortunately, what was left of my clothes I wore whilst expecting Theo were still around somewhere in a cardboard box.

Although no longer affected by someone's perfume, I now had to deal with the sweet smell of vinegar, sugar, onions, etc, which greeted me when Charles hugged me upon his return from work. He wore a cap and overalls, but somehow, the aroma got through. 'Shower, Mr Jones, please,' were my first words when he came through the door.

This pregnancy wasn't as easy as my first. I had a lively three-year-old to take care of and a part-time job. Nurse Wellington greeted me on my first appointment for a pre-natal check-up. 'Well, if it's not you again,' this time with a smile. 'Married yet?' 'No,' I grimaced. Why do I keep having to fend off this question? Well, my nurse and tea lady will be all of a flutter when they know Mr Jones will be back on the scene again. 'I have heard through the grapevine you have commandeered a fishing hut on Dungeness.' 'We have,' I replied through a wave of nausea. 'Sorry, I feel sick,' I flew to the toilets just in time. When I returned, any talk of marriage and fishing huts had been curtailed due to a very advanced labour being dealt with. I was weighed and had my blood pressure taken. I was told to eat ginger biscuits for my sickness and sent home. I decided to take a holiday from work. It was agreed as I hadn't had much time off since Theo was born. I was exhausted, happy, and contented in equal measure. Charles couldn't have any more time, so I decided to take Theo to the shack on my own. Charles wasn't too keen on us going without him but said he would come in the evenings to check up on us.

The bunk wasn't too comfortable but nowhere was with my growing bump. It was the peace and quiet I craved. We lived in a lively neighbourhood which normally suited us very well, but at the moment, it tired me. Somehow I felt drawn to this wooden home. It was where I felt the most contented. Despite the barren wasteland, I had peace of mind which I felt unable to find anywhere else.

We met Albert during our walks along the sand. Well, I walked; Theo toddled. He was mending his nets ready for the next day's fishing. He chatted to us asking if we would like some mackerel for our tea. He also mentioned how odd it seemed seeing the shack looking like a real home rather than the wreck it was. I explained I wasn't in any fit state to deal with gutting and cleaning. He said, 'Don't u'um worry, dearie, I can do it for yur.' He wandered over to the tap and washed the fish, lit a fire, and swung the cleaned mackerel over the flames on a pole. Theo was fascinated and couldn't take his eyes off Albert. We pulled the hot fleshy fish apart and ate with our fingers. Theo loved it. It was a new experience for both of us. 'Come back a'moro, dearie, an wi do it again if yur wannu,' Albert said. 'Yes, please,' I said, and couldn't wait to tell Charles about how kind Albert had been to us.

I loved the vast expanse of nothingness in front of us, the odd hut and rotting rowing boat at the water's edge.

I made us hot cocoa and poured mine into one of Carole's china cups she loved so much, Theo's into his plastic mug. Suddenly, in the cool night air, after Theo was tucked up fast asleep with his hot water bottle, I cried for my lost parents again. Hormones mixed with missing them so much and knowing they would never have the joy of being grandparents.

'Are you sure you are okay here?' Charles asked. He had come to visit for supper and brought some extra blankets. I tried to explain I needed the time to myself and how I craved the peace and quiet. I told him about Albert who had already said he would keep an eye on us. There were times when we all need this seclusion, and this was mine. Charles said he understood but worried about us. He also knew I wouldn't be here if I felt it was unsafe.

The next day, I decided Theo should learn to swim. I wanted to get him used to the water whilst we were here. Charles panicked somewhat the minute he came within yards of the sea, so I decided to try him in the chilly water for a while. He loved it laughing and shouting at the top of his voice. I realised not for the first time my son was only communicating when he was actually doing something constructive. When he started to shiver, I wrapped him in a bath towel and carried him back to the shack, singing away to him as I walked over the sand and gravel. I decided to take a walk around the area and have a proper look at some of the old buildings, the huge concrete listening ears built during the war. These were designed to pick up the sound of enemy aircraft through a stethoscope by an operator and gave the fifteen-minute warning of an impending attack. Not for the first time I realised what an interesting place this was. 'Supper, hot drink, hot water bottle, and bed for you, young man. Well done, today you will be swimming in no time.'

I had six weeks to go before my baby entered the world. I was back at work, and ready to be tucked under my desk and chair was a huge towel. 'We don't want a repeat of last time.' Sheila laughed. 'How is the model ship coming on?' I asked Mr I Can Do Anything . . . 'Okay, I think. It's a long and arduous job but will be well worth it. It seemed to be taking on a life of its own at the moment. One minute, I thought, 'Yes, we are nearly there,' and the next it fell apart.' The galleon he was working on when I left to have Theo sat in our wrecks department much admired by all who visit. He had done a fantastic job and the pride in his work was justified.

'How's my favourite girl?' Charles called as he came home from work one evening a few weeks later. I had not been too good all day and came home early. My baby had gone quiet, but for some reason, I felt heavy and uncomfortable. I had no benchmark to go on as this pregnancy was so different to the last one. Another two weeks to go, no more sickness, just a tiredness I couldn't shake off. Theo although a good child was sapping any spare energy I had. Keeping him entertained and busy was taking all my strength and ingenuity.

A couple of hours later, I started having twinges. 'I think this is it, Charles,' I said. I could not believe how quickly things accelerated from there. We had already arranged with Pat to take care of Theo and arrived at the hospital with me just about ready to push. 'Off you go, Mr Jones,' Nurse Wellington ordered. 'Go and sit down. I will come and get you when there is news. Right, young lady, let's get you sorted out.' I wanted to shout and cry out, but I didn't and at the same time, vowed I would never put myself through this again. Doctor Walker appeared and still looked sixteen. Phoebe arrived in a rush of water and mayhem. 'Well, here we are again, Mrs . . . sorry, Miss Connaught. A beautiful baby girl!' Charles appeared having been summoned by an overexcited Nurse Wellington. Still clutching his teacup, well, tea lady got wind of us coming back and couldn't wait to make sure Charles was taken care of and supplied with tea and this time a biscuit came with it.

'Oh my goodness!' he said. 'I cannot believe it, a little girl.'

'Say hello to Phoebe,' I said after he had hugged the breath out of me. We had decided on the name this time if we had a girl.

We were overjoyed to add Phoebe to our family. No stress about finding somewhere to live, just a beautiful dark-haired, blue-eyed little girl. Definitely Charles's colouring. I just hoped she wouldn't grow quite as tall as him. 'Six foot is too tall for a girl.' Well, I thought so anyway. Carole was small, so maybe she would take after her. How would she take to our uninhibited lifestyle and the shack? Theo was with our neighbour no doubt regaling her with stories of our times down on the beach which he hated and loved in equal measure. She hadn't quite got her head around why we chose to spend so much time there. I had invited her on a few occasions, but she politely declined. Sleeping in a bunk bed wasn't very appealing at my age was her excuse. 'You don't know what you are missing,' I teased.

'Oh, I think I do,' she cried.

Pat was first at the door to congratulate us, asking for a chance to hold our daughter. 'I really miss this,' she said wistfully. All Pat's children, four in total, had grown up and flown the nest. 'Well,' I said, 'between Theo and Phoebe, we can keep you occupied.' 'Come on in. I will make you some tea.' Pat led the way. Theo sat on her sofa reading a book about thunderbolts which happened during heavy storms. 'Hi,' he said as we walked in. 'Come and say hello to your new sister.' 'Hello, new sister,' he said, without looking up! Phoebe yawned. I know how she felt. Charles gently took hold of Theo's arm and pulled him up. 'That is no way to speak to Carrie now. Please be more polite.' 'Sorry,' he mumbled. 'That is good enough then,' Charles said. Theo very warily walked towards me peering at Phoebe under her blanket. 'I thought all babies were bald,' he said, touching Phoebe's head. 'She has masses of hair.' 'She may lose it,' I said. 'Sometimes it happens.' 'Well, I hope not for her sake,' he said. 'Who wants to grow up with no hair?' I smiled and said, 'It doesn't mean she won't have hair for the rest of her life. It is just something that happens. It will grow again very soon if she does lose it, and it will probably be of a different colour.'

Not quite so easy going back to work with two small children. I had started teaching Theo to read and write. He couldn't grasp the fundamentals. His mind was galloping on to another subject other than the one we were trying to get to grips with. I thought more than once about maybe registering him with the local school, but I wasn't too sure about his chances of fitting in. My patience was wearing very thin. Phoebe demanded a lot of attention. Theo had some other children to play with, but his interactive skills were non-existent. 'Life can be fun, Theo, if only you would just give it a try,' I thought in desperation.

I had more than one visit from the school inspector. I don't know why he bothered. All he seemed to do was tut and suck through his teeth. He was condescending and sometimes quite rude, but I had now become more determined to carry on teaching my son.

In between coming to the museum and times in the shack, Theo eventually got the idea about learning the basics.

Charles was still working hard for us all. Although Theo baffled him (me too if I wanted to be honest), he somehow seemed to find the answers with his son more readily than I could. 'He needs to be occupied all the time, Carrie. Sitting him down and teaching him one and one makes two bores him. He already knows that and wants to explore new things all the time.' Gardening albeit on a small scale pleased Theo. As he grew, he became more interested in planting flowers and vegetables, and Charles taught him to make cloches in plastic to cover our more delicate plants. He had his own little set of tools, a trowel and a fork, but that didn't stop him trying to use the bigger ones, getting in a paddy when Charles took them away from him.

What I hadn't realised was that Theo responded more to a simplistic view of things, which somehow I didn't understand. I was never too sure where to start with our lessons. I had the feeling he didn't either. I sometimes felt he was mocking me and my attempts to break through the invisible barrier I felt was there.

When we spent time in the shack, he would ask about the tides and why sometimes when we were here the water was close to the shoreline and then next time, it was a long way away. I tried to explain the moon's influence on our oceans but vowed to read up and learn more.

As the years passed by, I became more aware that home tutoring was best for my son. I didn't feel that sitting in a classroom was going to be useful for him. The one thing he was very good at was intolerance, and I knew he would switch off if the teacher wasn't talking directly to him or holding his interest. I imagined lots of detention and lines which made me smile.

Maybe if Theo hadn't been my first child, I would have been able to understand him better. I struggled, but with a grim determination, we built up a rapport, and I knew we would succeed in the end.

CHAPTER SEVEN
Carrie

'Theo, please don't whine, darling.' We had come to the shack for Theo's eighth birthday. He had got out of his bunk grumbling because we were not yet up and organised. Albert hadn't turned up today, so Theo was rather disappointed. We gave him his presents. Charles had made him a model aeroplane which he loved, and I had bought him some new clothes which he didn't. Phoebe had drawn him a card which he scrutinised quite closely before asking, 'What is it, Phebes?' She stood with her hands on her hips, legs akimbo, saying, 'If you don't know, I'm not telling you. It's a jelly fish she shouted to him. After breakfast of cereal and boiled eggs, we decided to walk in to town and have a look around the area. A cup of tea in a cafe and cake for Theo and Phoebe. 'So, you two, what's next? It's your choice Theo, as it's your birthday.' 'Anything but the shack,' he said in a morose voice. 'Do they have a library here?' 'I am sure they do,' I replied, quite taken aback for a moment, 'but we will need to join, I expect.' 'Well, we will do that then,' announced Theo. So library it is. The librarian stood in her check skirt and buttoned up cardigan, all official looking, probably wondering what the hell stood in front of her. 'We would like to join the library,' I said in uncertain tones. 'Really, all of you?' 'Not me,' Charles said. I could see a 'Oh that's a pity' look come over her round face and her cheeks redden. Her grey hair looked as if a pudding basin had been placed on her head and someone maybe herself had cut around it.

'I am going to be an astronaut,' announced Theo. 'Do you have anything on space exploration?' 'I'm sure we do, dear,' she said, sounding very patronising. 'We just need temporary tickets please. We are here on holiday.' 'Okay, that's fine. Names?' 'Carrie Connaught, Theo Jones, and Phoebe Jones.' I noticed she had put on a pair of glasses and peered over them with a questioning look on her face. 'Yes, they are our children, but I choose to keep my own name.' 'Really?' Mrs library lady said. 'How unusual?' She eyed us up and down once more and gave us our cards.

I felt her eyes piercing into my back as we wandered off to look around the shelves.

I decided on Dickens, *The Tale of Two Cities*, something in-depth and interesting. Theo went for something about planes and engines, mainly about the Spitfire. I didn't like to say he wouldn't understand it. I thought he could find that out for himself. I knew I would lose the argument. Phoebe chose Beatrix Potter. She wanted to look at the pictures as her reading skills were practically nil being so young. 'Charlie will read it to me,' she announced in a very grown-up and important way.

We wandered back to the shack with some sausages to barbecue, and some potatoes wrapped in foil to put in the fire. Charles lit the fire in the base of our makeshift barrel. We put some seaweed in with the wood which would enable it to smoulder rather that burn away. I split the sausages in half, so they cooked more easily. We left it all sizzling away and made hot drinks and sat on the steps watching the sun go down. Theo ran around pretending to fly his plane making something like aircraft noises to add authenticity. Phoebe cuddled up to Charles looking at the pictures in her book. Much later, the night drew in, darkness was falling, hot water bottles in bunks, full of sausages, jacket potatoes, baked beans, and a birthday cake which I had made and brought with us along with eight candles. We fell into our bunks tired but happy. 'Night, night, everyone.' Charles had other ideas. When he was sure Theo and Phoebe were asleep, he came down to my bunk and snuggled up and kissed me on my neck, then my breasts, and worked his way down. We went outside in to the cool night air and made love on the beach, We laid on the sand and listened to the sounds of the night, mainly a drone from the light house, the squawk of some late night gull chasing a fishing trawler, hoping for a treat thrown in desperation from a fisherman trying to ward of the noisy creature. I knew without doubt, I had conceived Jack that night.

The following day, Albert appeared and gave Theo a model of a seagull with a fish in its mouth carved out of driftwood. 'Sorry, I not 'ere for ur birfday, lad. Missus wasn't too good, and I 'ad to take her to the docs. She be okay tho' just a bit o' tummy trouble.' 'I am glad she is all right,' I said to Albert. 'We missed you, but we do have some cake left for you. Would you like a sandwich, Albert?' 'I have just had some for lunch. I be all right ta, missus, we got somat all ready at 'ome.' 'Please say thank you to Albert, Theo.' 'Thank you very much, Albert.' I could see by the look on his face Theo loved his present.

Phoebe nudged up to Albert and gave him one of her winning smiles. 'Well, wha' 'ave we got 'ere.' Albert laughed. From behind his back, he produced a kite. 'Wow, thank you, Albert. Come on everybody let's have a go with this,' Charles shouted. 'You carry on, lad. I best get back to the missus.' 'I will get you some cake to take home, Albert.' I went to the tin and cut some cake for Albert and his wife. 'See you, tomorrow.' I loved this old man of the sea and felt highly honoured to know him.

Charles hoisted Phoebe on to his shoulders and ran with her flying her kite as they went. We had a glorious couple of hours, before we went back to our wooden home and collapsed on the beach, laughing and rolling around like demented puppies. Supper of baked beans and a crusty loaf, followed by what was left of the birthday cake, and we were ready to clear up and have a swill down.

Theo was the first, and we all had to go outside whilst he got ready for bed. Then I washed Phoebe and myself and Charles followed.

The wind was particularly strong that night and whistled around our shack for what seemed like hours. I couldn't sleep and listened to the sounds of my family. Phoebe sucking her thumb, Charles quietly grunting to himself, and Theo shifting about on a rustling comic which he had fallen asleep reading. I had already got out of my bunk and switched his torch off but couldn't rescue the comic without waking him.

We had a boat ride planned for Sunday. Albert was going to organise a trip out to sea to watch the seals. Phoebe was very excited.

Theo was nonplussed, and Charles thought he might be seasick. Me? Well, I suppose I was in the excited category.

We had a ropey old camera which let us down on various occasions. Our photographs were usually a blurred mess, but we would have another go with the new film which they had put in for us in the shop. The assistant said to take the camera back when the film was used up and not attempt to take it out of the camera ourselves. Apparently, we let in too much light and spoilt our photographs!

I felt quite comfortable risking life and limb with this solid-looking vessel. 'Righto, life jackets on, everyone. My name is Stan. I am a friend of Albert, and I am your tour guide for the day,' he joked.

We boarded and kitted ourselves out as requested and settled down to enjoy the trip. 'Is Albert coming with us?' I asked. 'No, he doesn't go out on a boat unless there is something to bring in at the end of the day. He never sails for pleasure. Says it's a waste of time, besides which he sees enough of the rolling waves anyway.'

At the mention of rolling waves, Charles looked a bit green. Phoebe thought the whole thing an adventure. 'Will we see Moby Dick?' she asked in between bouncing in the harness Stan had attached her to and waving to the occupants of a passing boat. 'I bloody well hope not,' Charles said. 'Please don't swear in front of the children, Charles.' 'Sorry, just thought anything bigger than a gold fish might tip this thing over.'

'Right,' Theo said, 'when do we get to see the seals?' 'Anytime now, lad. Keep your eyes peeled. This is fertile fishing ground, so they should be hereabouts.' 'There, look,' Phoebe shouted. Sure enough, a large group were playing and displaying their talents of the fish catching variety. 'Wow!' said Theo. 'They are magnificent!' 'Good heavens!' a reaction like that from my son shocked me, but there again he was actually doing something albeit from a boat, which even for me was tossing about like a cow pat in a river. 'Where have I heard that before!'

Charles had gone very quiet. 'Are you okay?' I shouted over the engine. 'Fine, just fine. Remind me, I'm a landlubber next time anyone suggests I get in boat.'

We spent some time watching the seals playing. It was as if they knew they had an audience and were determined to show off to their viewing public.

We had taken sandwiches which no one fancied except Stan. He devoured most of them in the space of a few minutes. 'Thank you. They were great,' he said, wiping his mouth with a not-too-clean hankie.

We arrived back on terra firma, and even I had a problem standing up straight. I felt drunk. We thanked Stan for his time and lessons on the fishing and mating habits of the seals. Theo and Phoebe ran off the minute we got back. 'Where are you off to now?' 'I am going to find Albert,' Theo shouted back at me to tell him how awesome the seals were.

'Don't be long,' I muttered to myself as I staggered up the beach to the shack. 'Phew,' I said as I slumped on the wooden step. 'Phew yourself,' Charles said, 'don't do that to me again!' 'You didn't have to come.' 'What and look silly in front of everyone?' he said with meaning.

Theo came running back hotly followed by Phoebe. 'Albert's not there, so we will have to thank him another day.'

'Okay a cup of tea and then home. I will drive, Charles. You look done in.'

'I am fine, Carrie. Don't fuss.' Where have I heard that before?

It was Sunday evening and time to go back to our house and reality. As usual Pat was there to help us unload and make us a very welcome cup of tea. Theo showed off his present from Albert, and Phoebe was busy unravelling her kite strings which had become tangled. I warned her they would when she wouldn't let Charles fold it properly. Never mind, it's all part of a learning curve and will keep her occupied till bedtime which was fast approaching. 'We saw seals today, Pat. They were so happy playing in the sea,' Phoebe said with wonder in her voice. 'They are sooooooo good at catching fish.' 'Well, it is just as well because that's what they live on,' Pat said, giving her a hug. 'I know, but they are very clever. No Moby Dick though,' she said sadly.

'Thank god for that,' Charles muttered, still looking a funny shade of grey/green.

Monday morning. How the nights sped by so quickly at home but seemed to go on forever in the shack. Theo and Phoebe sat in front of me, expectation in their eyes. 'Well, what is it to be today?' I asked. 'I need to do more Maths,' Theo said. 'I want Rupert the Bear,' said Phoebe. So Phoebe sat with her book whilst I went through the wonders of algebra, fractions, and trigonometry with Theo. We had reached the stage where he was practically teaching me. He had inherited my love of figures and apart from being fidgety wanting to do something far more interesting (that's for Charles), we did very well. The school inspector was still tutting and sucking his teeth but had to admit we were doing well. He couldn't help but be impressed by Theo's knowledge and Phoebe's reading ability. She managed to fool him as she had me, making up a story as she went along from the pictures in her book.

'Right, it is my afternoon in the museum, so we had better wind up the lessons and get going before I am sacked.' 'What's sacked?' Phoebe asked. 'Well, it means you are told to leave your work because the big bad boss doesn't think you are capable.' 'Okay,' she looked down at her shoes as if to say I still don't know what you mean. I gave my daughter a hug and hoped she would never have to face dismissal from any job. I hoped none of my children ever saw a dark cloud, although, of course, they would because that's life.

'Oh not again,' Sheila and Mary teased a couple of months later. 'Let us know when to bring out the towel.' I felt different this time. Not so sick, had boundless energy, and also more excited to know I was having another child. 'This will be it, Charles,' I had said on many occasions over the last few weeks. 'We cannot afford any more children. Is that right?' Charles said, 'I thought you said I was irresistible.' 'Well, maybe you are, Charles Jones, but this really is it.' Unfortunately, Charles was ageing rather well. His black hair tinged with grey only enhanced his looks and appeal. Me, I looked ragged around the edges, and a lot more than the two years older. The maternity wear I had before was well and truly worn out. 'We will get new, Charles,' said. 'Let's hope Doris Day is not in fashion any more and we have a choice,' he teased. I was reluctant to spend too much as I have said this was the final child. As I reached the seventh month, I was still able to fit in to some of my loser clothes. I treated myself to a decent haircut. My mousy blonde locks had grown below my shoulders, and I thought it aged me. 'A bob it is,' I said to the hairdresser who was waving her scissors in anticipation. I chose the style from a picture on the wall in the salon. I knew I would never look like the model, but I would have a damned good try.

'Oops, wrong house!' Charles said when he came home from work. 'Can you tell me where Miss Caroline Connaught lives, please? I seem to have lost the love of my life.' With that, Charles picked me up and swung me round forgetting for a moment I was heavily pregnant. 'Well, that did the back a lot of good.' He clutched his sides in mock pain. 'Do you like it?' I asked. 'I do. It is just a bit of a shock, that's all.' 'It will be easier to manage with three children to care for and educate,' I said more to myself.

'We hope this is it,' the governors and trustees of the museum said drily when I said I would be off with another baby shortly. We were having a meeting about where we could go next with our exhibitions. 'Look,' I said. 'We have a room at the back which we don't use. We did have some bits and pieces awaiting restoration in there, but our very talented, creative Mr Miller, him of the I can do anything . . . sort had not only restored said items but had helped us to place them strategically through the museum. Why don't we turn it in to a tea room?' I suggested. 'I expect between Sheila, Mary, and me, we can make a few cakes and organise tea and coffee.' 'Well, that's all well and good, Carrie,' the boss-eyed, toady-looking treasurer said, 'you will be off again soon which will leave everything to the rest of us.' I held my hands up in surrender. 'Okay, just a thought. Wait till I come back if you like. I am sure Charles will help with the decorating along with Mr Miller.' I knew it would be awhile before the tea room was up and running. New ideas do not sit well on the trustees' shoulders. I hadn't realised at the time just how long it would take!

'Phew,' I exhaled out in the fresh air, 'that was a meeting and a half.' Sheila was outside with her Rothman Kingsize blowing smoke rings and chewing gum. I told her about the cafe idea. 'Well done, you,' she said in between coughs. 'Fantastic idea, but I am not the best cake maker in the world.' 'That is the least of our worries, Sheila. We have to persuade the trustees to go for it first. They were not too keen, but I hope to win them around.' 'Well, if anyone can do it, you can, Carrie.'

'Ouch,' I said as I leant against the wall, 'that was one hell of a kick custard.' My bumps all had names after the food I fancied whilst pregnant. Theo was pickled onion; Phoebe was apple or gooseberry.

'You all off to the shed this weekend?' Mary asked when I went back in with Sheila. 'I expect we will have one last hurrah before this little one arrives,' I said, knowing that was where this baby was conceived made me smile.

Well, she was still here, Nurse Wellington. The familiarity of the maternity ward seemed somehow comforting through my labour pains. I really struggled this time. 'What's keeping you, custard!' I said through excruciating backache and gasps of gas and air. 'The baby will be here when it's ready . . .' She couldn't help herself, our Nurse Wellington. 'Do I still call you, "Miss" Connaught?' She stressed the 'miss'. 'If you like,' I panted, 'or Carrie will do.' By now, I knew her and the doctor (who had aged slightly, thank goodness!) quite well. His youthful looks had been unnerving to say the least.

This was the longest labour I had been through. I knew Charles would be pacing the floor in the corridor. This time he did have a choice: he could be with me, but he declined. I understood and didn't really want an audience even if it was Charles. Also I could tell you, he would have got his life history had he been in the room and a death wish to go with it!

Jack burst on to the scene six hours after I arrived at the hospital. I was so exhausted. I didn't feel the elation I had previously. 'Congratulations, you have another son, Miss Connaught!'

'Wonderful!' I said and promptly passed out. I came round with an anxious face close to mine, blue eyes staring at me through a mist of tears. 'Oh god, Carrie, I thought we had lost you!' Charles was beside himself. Nurse Wellington came into her own again. 'Don't worry, Mr Jones. These things happen from time to time, your wif . . . sorry, Miss Connaught's blood pressure dropped rapidly, but it is back to normal now. We will take baby so you can rest. Does he have a name?' 'Jack,' I said through a haze of weariness. 'That's it, Jack,' Charles confirmed.

A bump and crash through the ward door heralded the arrival of Mrs Tea Trolley. 'Oh, hello again.' She simpered looking at Charles as if he was the last man on earth. 'Would you like some tea? And what did you have this time?' 'A son,' I said. 'How lovely!' she said, staring straight in to Charles's eyes. I felt like saying, 'You don't stand a chance, you batty old woman.' Instead, I meekly asked for tea too. Charles and I enjoyed a few precious minutes alone with our tea. 'That was tough,' I said through tears. 'I know I said no more children, but I really mean no more! In fact, no more of anything.' 'Do I come into that category then?' Charles asked. 'For the time being you do, Mr Jones.' 'Oh, tea lady, it is then! I will go and give her the good news!' At this moment in time, I couldn't even argue on that one. 'Just joking, Carrie,' Charles stuttered. 'Oh really, that's a shame then!' Charles looked at me with worry still showing in his eyes and tears fell again. He stood up shuffling his feet, hugged me, and said he would go and let Pat know our good news and leave me to rest. 'Theo and Phoebe will be wanting to know if they have a brother or sister too.'

Charles looked even more tired than I did. He had sat by me for hours. I had slept fitfully and had begun to feel better. 'Please try and get an early night,' I said to him as he bent to kiss me. 'Maybe Pat will keep Theo and Phoebe for us tonight.'

Theo liked the idea of a brother but said the age difference wouldn't exactly make them playmates – the kind of response I had expected from him. Phoebe was far happier being the only girl. What fun this would be when Jack grew up!

'Well, Miss, is this it then?' Nurse Wellington asked as she brought Jack in for his morning feed. 'Hello, darling,' I said. Nurse W gave me a strange look. 'Not you.' I laughed. 'I should hope not. I might be a spinster but definitely the heterosexual type.' 'Pleased to hear it,' I said as I took Jack in my arms. For some reason, he didn't seem to resemble either Charles or me. He yawned and briefly opened his eyes which were navy blue, somewhat darker than Charles and Phoebe's. His little red face reminded me of an elderly uncle I once had. The double chin lent itself to a slight resemblance to Aunt Maude. 'Oh dear!' Here I go again, tears flowing as I thought of Maude, John, and Carole. How much they would all have loved my children, although I couldn't see how I would have persuaded any of them to visit the shack! It suddenly dawned on me the remoteness I saw in Theo was a hint of Carole. We both loved the finer things in life like tea in a bone china cup, although like Charles and myself didn't have much money. I remember her saying to me once, 'Even if you only have a penny to your name, spend it wisely.' I knew I was loved by my parents. I wish I had had more time with them. Well, what happened, happened. Maybe I wouldn't have got to university or met Charles, who knows? I don't think Carole would be quite as persistent as Maude about education.

Jack munched on my breast which made we wince slightly. He is so much hungrier than either Theo or Phoebe were. I felt and saw my tears drop on his head. 'Come on, Carrie. This won't do,' I sternly spoke to myself. I eventually managed to stop and felt happier when I thought about introducing Jack to our 'holiday home' and Albert. Besides I didn't want nurse to see me in this state. I knew beneath her tough exterior beat a heart of gold, but slight abruptness tinged with some caring words wouldn't help at the moment.

'Well, you are in for an interesting time,' were the first words Theo spoke to Jack. 'Carrie and Charlie are mad.' 'Oh really?' I said. 'Is that mad as in insane or mad as in fun.' 'A bit of both,' he replied.
'Thank you, son. I will be home soon to continue classes. I hope you and Phoebe are doing the homework I set you. The last thing I want at the moment is the tut, tutting school inspector tut tutting even louder, and if he sucks his dentures any more, they will fall out.' 'We are,' Phoebe said, gazing fondly at her baby brother.

Charles picked us up from hospital a week later. My house shone like a new pin. Pat was there to greet us with a cup of tea and a homemade casserole. Where would I be without her? I was bordering on tears again but kept them in check this time. I noticed for the first time Pat looked weary. 'Are you okay?' I asked, putting my hand on her arm. 'Yes, I think so,' she said. 'I am so lucky to have you all. I hardly see my family and to be honest, I couldn't cope with the loneliness if you were not here.'

'Well, we will be introducing Jack to the shack soon when it gets a bit warmer. Please say you will come.'
'Oh, I don't know.'
'Oh, go on, Pat. You haven't lived until you have tasted food from our makeshift barbecue. It is usually well done to burn. Just to warn you,' Theo muttered.
'Please don't smirk like that, Theo. It is very rude.'
'Sorry, Carrie, I didn't mean to sound rude. It is just an observation. Of course, it is Theo, silly me.'

Phoebe was more interested in whether she could take her kite rather than anything else. 'You will love Albert,' she said through a mask of chocolate cake Pat had made. Pat had heard us talk about Albert and agreed very reluctantly to accompany us when we went to the shack next time.
'It will be a squash in the car,' Charles said. 'I hadn't thought about that,' I said. 'Don't worry,' Pat whispered, because Jack had gone to sleep in her arms. 'I will follow in my car.' Looking at Pat's shiny mini, I didn't think she would be too pleased when she saw the state of the drive up to our shack. 'Park on the road, Pat, and we will fetch you down to the shack.'

Pat's rosy cheeks belied her tiredness. 'Oh my goodness, I can see why you love it here!' She sat on the steps looking out to sea watching Albert's boat fade on the horizon wondering why she felt so worn out.
'Come on, Pat. It's the customary cricket match time.'
'Oh, I would rather not, Theo, if you don't mind.'

Charles sat beside her and put his arm across her shoulders, a move that would have most women wilting. Pat had always appeared immune to his looks and charm. She had talked about her husband who deserted her some years earlier for a younger model and said on more than one occasion that she had lost faith in men, which was understandable I suppose. I knew I couldn't bear it if that happened to me. She was left with four young children to bring up, all of whom seemed unaware of the hardship she suffered and sacrifices she made. I don't think they were selfish. I know they had very busy lives and did not realise how lucky they were to have her. In all the time we have lived next door, I don't think I had seen any of them more than once or twice. 'Kite please,' Phoebe interrupted my thoughts. Pat had fallen asleep on Charles's shoulder, so I took Phoebe off down the beach to fly her kite. Theo was making something out of wood, with a penknife he had borrowed from Charles, to give Albert when he came back. It looked a bit strange, but I didn't like to ask what it was. Jack was asleep tucked under his blanket in the Moses basket, which I had to say had seen better days now on its third child. We spent a few happy hours just talking, playing cricket, and even managed an improvised a game of rounders.

After a cup of hot chocolate and biscuits, we decided to pack up and go home to get Jack ready for his bath and bed.

Theo was disappointed as Albert hadn't come back. 'Never mind,' I said. 'We will see him next time.'

'But I wanted to give him this.' He laid a carving of a little rowing boat in my hand along with two carefully carved miniature oars.

'Let's leave it in the shack, and we can give it to him next weekend.'

I was so proud of what Theo had made. He really needed to be doing something all the time. The little boat had gone through various stages as Theo carved it. At one time, I thought it was a slipper. Then, I began to see the boat emerge. 'Albert will love it,' I said to him, brushing his hair out of his eyes, which annoyed him immensely as you would expect.

'Good night, Pat,' we all said together. 'Thank you for a lovely day,' she said. I didn't like to say she had spent best part of it asleep on Charles's shoulder. 'See you soon,' I said, as she unlocked her front door. An hour later, Pat phoned to say she didn't feel well. I went round to see her and realised she was having trouble breathing. I immediately called an ambulance. She was taken in to hospital. As I waved her off, I said, 'We would come and see her as soon as possible.' I felt relieved to know she was in good hands, although I just hoped we hadn't contributed to her illness insisting she came to the shack.

'Here come the tribe.' Mary laughed when I went back to work with all three in tow. I was really concerned for Pat, but I had to get back and supplement our income. I set Theo and Phoebe tasks and put Jack behind my desk in his Moses basket.

Sometime later, I found out that Pat was okay. She had a slight heart problem and had been given some beta blockers to help and could be discharged tomorrow. 'It is my turn to have a cooked meal and a full teapot ready,' I said, as I welcomed her back home. 'Please don't give us another fright like that, Pat.'

'I will try not to,' she murmured. I tucked her up in bed and asked if she would like me to call anyone. As was typical of her, Pat said, 'No, I don't want to worry anybody.'

'Right, I will be in to see you in the morning.'

We already had keys to each other's houses, so I wouldn't have a problem getting in to see her. I made sure her phone was in easy reach and said, 'Just call if you need us.' Charles was upset because he thought we had caused this. The doctor reassured him and said this had been coming on for some time. 'Just a glitch,' he said. 'Everything should be fine now.'

I made a mental note not to ask Pat to take care of my children too often now. I knew she wouldn't be up to it for some time. She had a scare and needed to recover quietly. It was a fine line to draw because Pat loved my children. I needed to help her understand that it was more a case of not wanting to tire her out rather than we think she wasn't capable which would do more damage to her health and well-being.

I popped in to see her the next day. She had a lot more colour and said she felt so much better. 'Can you do me a small favour, Carrie? Can I borrow one of your lovely china cups? I cannot face my tea in a mug at the moment.' That surprised me. Pat liked builder's tea, thick and strong, loaded with sugar; however, now she wanted weak tea, with no sugar, and a china cup. 'Of course, Pat, I will go and get one for you and make you a pot of tea before I go to work.' I returned with a cup which had ivy leaves painted all around the rim, one of my favourites, and made her tea. 'Oh, I meant to say I don't like ivy, Carrie!' Pat said with her glint in her eye and a smile on her lips. 'Thank goodness, she has her sense of humour back!'

'Please ask Theo and Phoebe to come and see me so they know I am okay,' Pat requested.
'Of course, we will come and see you later. Bye for now.'

After work, I needed to do some tutorials with Theo and Phoebe. Our lessons had been thin on the ground recently. Theo could read and work on his Maths on his own, but Phoebe needed encouragement to sit down and learn her tables. I had also set her a task to find all the different countries in the world with her globe and to write down as many as she found along with those that border each other. A tough call for a six-year-old, but it kept her occupied for some time.

After lessons, we called on Pat with Jack asleep in my arms. 'Well, here they are,' she said, patting the top of Phoebe's head. 'How are my two favourite children? Sorry, Jack, three.' 'We are fine, Pat,' Theo answered. 'So glad you are feeling better.'
'Thank you, Theo. You sound so grown-up.'
'Well, I am,' he said. 'I know,' Pat agreed, winking at me.
'Charles is working late, but I am sure he will be around later smelling of vinegar.'
'Ha, ha, tell him not to worry. He will probably be very tired after a long day. Please tell him I know he is thinking of me, but I am okay.'
'Come on, Pat.' I laughed. 'Most women would give anything for a few moments alone with Charles.'
'Go on with you, Carrie Connaught. He is not my type.'

'Well, you are the first.' We burst in to fits of giggles much to Theo's disgust.

'One day, the ladies will be fighting over your son, not if I have anything to do with it, Carrie.'

'Why would I be interested in girls? I want to go to university and make something of my life.'

'Oh really?' I said. 'You can do both, you know?'

'If you say so,' he muttered under his breath.

'Well, we will leave that door open then,' I thought to myself.

CHAPTER EIGHT
Carrie and Jack

Christ Church College, Oxford, 1973. Theo Jones was studying Biology, Chemistry, and the Sciences. Carrie talked about the long road leading to his place at one of the most prestigious universities. He was safely installed in the Halls of Residence along with a couple of other scholarship winners. By now, he could be classed as tall, fair, and handsome, and even if I say so myself somewhat clever.

Carrie wrote her life had changed dramatically since the early days of home schooling. She also said that in a surprising way, Charles was the catalyst leading to this scenario. He recognised more than I did about what kept Theo's attention and sparked his interest. Between us we got him here. Even though Theo was dismissive of his own brilliance, he had a kind of arrogance which did not endear him to his peers. I felt he had built a wall around himself which was only penetrable by those he wanted to let in. Carole came in to my thoughts again. I remembered her being very similar.

Carrie and Charlie said goodbye to Theo with a heavy heart. 'Please be off now,' their son had said. His demeanour hadn't mellowed over the years. 'We love you, darling,' I said as I hugged him. 'Please let us know if you need anything.'

'I will be absolutely fine, Carrie. I will make you both proud of me.'

'We already are, son,' I said with very moist eyes. 'Don't cry, Carrie,' I reprimanded myself inwardly. Our son would be embarrassed and that was the last thing we wanted. 'Bye, son,' Charles said as he shook Theo's hand. An odd display of affection, but this was how they greeted each other and said goodbye. I found it quite touching in a way. They appeared to be strangers, albeit very close strangers if that was possible.

Finally, Theo was where he needed to be. I was very surprised he wrote home still after his second year telling us about his life at Oxford. We compared notes about my time there. All of a sudden, he became less egotistical and even asked how often we visited the shack. We said we had planned to spend Christmas there if we didn't get snow. Phoebe was spending time with friends, and we had invited one of Jack's friends. Theo was doing well as we knew he would, but I sensed a kind of ennui in his letters which seemed reflected in his words. I phoned to ask him if he was okay. He just said, 'It's nothing, Carrie. I just feel very tired.' Charles said we would visit Theo at the weekend; however, Theo was very apprehensive as he didn't want a lot of fuss. For once, we insisted. I said we needed to put our minds at rest as we were very concerned for him.

The minute I saw my son, I knew something was wrong. 'Have you seen a doctor?' I asked. 'Yes, he just said I had been overdoing it and needed to rest.' Apart from his studies, Theo had a job in a local pub.

It took us at least two hours to persuade Theo to let us take him to hospital. We went to the Radcliffe Infirmary on the Woodstock Rd for some reassurance. We managed to park in the front car park quite easily, which was just as well as neither Charles nor I had mastered the art of parking in a small space.

The nurse in Accident and Emergency took one look at Theo and hastened him through triage to see a consultant. After several hours and a lot of tests, we were told he had an ulcerated stomach which had bled. He was going to need surgery immediately. 'Please wait whilst we try to find an empty theatre.' I was so scared, but, at the same time, relieved to know what the problem was. 'Have you eaten much today?' the nurse asked him. 'No,' Theo replied. 'I haven't had much of an appetite.' Even though he was ill, Theo managed to look bored and disinterested in his surroundings.

He was being his usual philosophical self. I could tell he was worried though. We had been assured he would be okay, but I felt sick with worry. Charles was as pale as Theo. I knew he was terribly worried too but staying strong for us. We sat around the trolley which Theo was laying on, trying to be confident and reassuring to him.

Finally, I could recognise my son. His attitude was a mixture of bravado and pride. 'Please let your guard down,' I pleaded to him in my head.

After what seemed like hours which it probably was, Theo was wheeled back to recovery. He had had major surgery, but he had more colour in his cheeks and looked more like himself than the pale shadow we had brought to the hospital.

Theo's nurse was saying that he was a very lucky man to have survived so long with the internal bleeding and pain. She had a comforting presence in her starched apron and cap and an efficient and smart manner. Somehow though, her words seemed to echo through my head as I waited for our son to emerge from the anaesthetic.

As we sat waiting, I looked at this old establishment that was our Infirmary, miles and miles of corridors which had distinct smells and a somehow comforting ambience not prevalent in more modern hospitals. Even though the walls were covered in large white tiles, some cracked and chipped, the wards were spotlessly clean and smelt of disinfectant.

I had spent time in here during my Oxford years when I had my tonsils out and woke up to find the formidable Maude staring at me. 'Ice cream and jelly for you for a while,' she said in her usual authoritative manner. I remember thinking at the time, 'How are you feeling, dear?' would have been nice. It was funny how thoughts pop in to your head when the relief was overtaken by memories. I started thinking about the time I met Charles in the pub garden opposite the hospital. Who would have thought that we would have a son who would win a place at Oxford. Charles glanced at me with a weak smile, relief written all over his face. We phoned Pat from the pay phone in the corridor to let Phoebe and Jack know what was happening. I was stupid enough to cry when she answered which for a split second made Pat catch her breath thinking something dreadful happened. I explained about Theo's operation and asked that she let Phoebe and Jack know he was okay and we were waiting for him to come round. 'They have gone shopping for me,' Pat said. 'They were restless, and I didn't want to leave the phone.'

'Please tell them not to worry, and I will call again later when we have more information.'

I cannot believe how lucky we were to reach Theo in time and to have the kind and caring staff to look after us. We sat down again by Theo's bed. I knew enough about hospitals not to be too worried about the tubes and wires attached to my son. They are a necessary evil after an operation.

I was distracted by a voice asking, 'Cup of tea, dear?' 'Oh yes, please,' I mumbled. As I turned to see the tea lady, I realised she was looking at Charles. 'And what about you, love?' she asked as she tore her eyes away and addressed me. I smiled to myself. 'Tea please. Milk, no sugar.' Charles's tea was placed gently on the little table; mine was plonked down, some of which ended up in the saucer.

Theo began to stir, and I grabbed his hand and spoke softly to him, saying, everything went well and he would feel much better soon. Charles went to find a doctor and came back saying someone would be here soon to check on our son.

A white-coated apparition appeared about an hour later. 'Theo lost a lot of blood,' he explained, 'but he is young and strong, and after a transfusion, which we will set up now, he should recover very quickly. His duodenum was quite ulcerated, which is strange in one so young. I think a mixture of diet and stress is responsible. Some students push themselves too hard. Drinking, the wrong food, and not a lot of sleep take their toll. They rebel a little being away from home, and it catches up on them.' I didn't have the energy to explain our son wouldn't need to be a rebel, besides which it would sound a bit feeble to try and explain. It was more likely to be his adopted lifestyle which was to blame.

We were fortunate to be given a room in the hospital so we could stay for a few days. Charles wandered off down St Giles to find a chemist to get us toothpaste, brushes, flannel, and soap.

'Well, young man, you were lucky,' twittered the young nurse as she attached him to a drip and blood supply. 'How many times was I going to hear that today?'

All of a sudden, a young lady rushed in to the room. 'What on earth have you been up to, Tiger's Eyes,' she addressed Theo. 'Oh hello,' I said, 'I have never heard my son called that before.' 'Sorry, I'm Amelia. Milly for short.' 'Carrie,' I introduced myself. 'I have heard a lot about you, Carrie, and very pleased to meet you.' Theo managed a quiet hi to Milly who immediately sat in the seat Charles had vacated and proceeded to talk nineteen to the dozen. She seemed rather daunting in her multicoloured sweater, long skirt, and equally colourful socks tucked in to her Doc Martens. Her hair was flame red and a mass of wild Pre-Raphaelite curls tamed by a colourful hairclip resembling a peacock, the clip that is not her. 'We are a kind of item,' Milly said directly to me. 'Is that so?' I said. 'Theo has never mentioned you.' Theo almost smiled. The scene probably amused him and helped with the pain he must be feeling. 'You have been found out, Theo,' I accented his name, which seemed to be wasted on both Theo and Milly. They were staring at each other, and by the look on their faces were rather hoping to be alone.

Charles appeared with a carrier bag holding our toiletries and I hope some food. Before I had a chance to open my mouth, Milly was up and shaking Charles's hand and introducing herself.

'I have got you some fruit, Theo, and a bottle of squash. If you want or need anything else, let us know,' Charles said in a quiet voice. 'We need to find a jug with some water,' Milly announced and went off in cloud of colour which was every hue of the rainbow. She came back shortly with the jug and lightly kissed Theo on the forehead. 'There you are, Tiger's Eyes. Let me know if you would like a drink.' 'We need to check that first with the nurse,' I said tentatively. 'Of course, I hadn't thought of that,' Milly said with a startled look on her pretty face.

'Come on, Charles. Let's leave these two to spend some time together. We can phone Pat and speak to Jack and Phoebe.' (Yes, our faithful old war horse had come to the rescue again.) She had insisted on looking after Jack even though Phoebe was around to keep an eye on things and hopefully find some food. 'What the hell was that?' Charles squeaked, referring to Milly. 'Theo's girlfriend, apparently,' I said. The look on Charles's face was one of incredulity. 'Really?' he said. 'Are you sure?'

'Well, she told me they are an item or kind of. Maybe we can ask Theo when we visit him later.' Even as I said it, I knew interrogation wouldn't sit comfortably with Theo, besides which it wasn't important. I just wanted him well.

'Hi, Pat. It's Carrie. I hope Jack hasn't worn you out. Everything here is looking much better. Theo has come round, although a little sleepy, which is to be expected. He is having a blood transfusion, and we will need to stay a couple of nights.'

'That's fine,' Pat said. I spoke to Phoebe and Jack. Their voices cheered me, and when I said we were staying a while and Theo was out of the woods, they were very happy to be with Pat who of course would love them and look after them like her own. 'Well, we will just go on being spoiled rotten then,' Jack said. 'And you will have to pick up the pieces when you get back, Carrie. I am pleased Theo is okay.' 'Thank you, Jack. We will call you tomorrow. Love you.' 'Love you too,' Jack whispered down the phone in an embarrassed tone. I smiled to myself as I replaced the receiver.

The pub had a different landlord. The bench we occupied all those years ago long gone along with all the others. In their places were bistro tables and chairs. It was a warm autumnal evening. We elected to sit outside to get some air. 'What a day!' Charles picked a late flowering rose and handed it to me saying, 'I think I love you, Carrie Connaught. Is that right?' I laughed. Two pints and chicken in the basket sat in front of us and we could now relax knowing our son was out of danger.

I now knew why when the university 'went down' at the end of the Michaelmas term, Theo had opted to spend time with his friends, namely Milly!

Charles phoned work the next morning to say he would be back later in the week. His boss didn't sound too keen on the idea, but Charles said his son came first. 'Oh yes, of course, Charlie,' he demurred. 'Take what time you need,' realising he had overstepped the mark a little.

I phoned Sheila who just said with a wry tone to her voice, 'Please don't worry, Carrie. You are not indispensible.' Followed by, 'Don't be too long. We cannot manage without you.' 'Which is it?' I laughed. 'Oh, you know Caroline Connaught only too well.' 'Bye for now. Hope Theo continues to make good progress. We are thinking of you.'

After a fitful night's sleep, Charles and I went to see Theo. He was sat up in bed looking so much better drinking a cup of tea. 'Sorry about all this, Carrie and Charlie. I promise to look after myself much better in the future.' 'We hope so,' we said in unison. 'Please don't scare us again. We will stay another night and then come back when you are discharged to bring you home to recuperate.' I offered to speak to his tutors, but he said he would do that himself. 'I don't really need to come home, Carrie. I will be fine.'

'Oh no, you won't, Tiger's Eyes. Do as you are told for a change.' Coloured jumper and woolly socks had arrived looking like she had slept in her clothes. 'Okay, okay, hands up. I am outnumbered.' 'Can I come too?' Milly asked. 'I want to see the shack Theo speaks about.'

'Well, I will speak to Phoebe and see how she feels about sharing. We only have three bedrooms. Jack and Theo will be okay. He has two single beds in his room.' The look between Theo and Milly told me they were not happy being in separate rooms. My house, my rules flitted through my mind. I didn't know this girl well enough to condone her sleeping with my son under my roof. I promised Milly we would spend a day in the shack but staying there overnight was out of the question with Theo needing to be comfortable. We had also arranged for a nurse to come in twice a week to check on him and change his dressings. Given her manner which was brisk and efficient, I think she would hyperventilate at the thought of Theo sleeping in a bunk in a shack in the middle of nowhere.

Charles said his boss had been more than amenable on his return to work and very concerned about Theo and our family. Everyone who worked on the line for Charles asked how his son was. 'No going to that shed of yours for a while then,' a blue turbaned woman shouted. 'That's my business,' Charles had snorted. 'Sorry, didn't mean to offend. Me pinny is mucky. I'm off to change it.' Charles knew she was going outside for a sly cigarette but didn't say anything. 'Don't be long, Vera,' he shouted after her. 'I won't, boss,' she called back. Vera was one of many of his charges working on the line. They seemed to enjoy themselves and worked hard to meet production targets. A short break for a ciggie didn't interfere too much with Charles's schedule of works.

A few days later, Theo phoned to say he was being discharged. 'Don't worry, Charles. I will go and fetch them.' What the neighbours, Pat in particular, would make of Milly was anyone's guess. You would think, given our lifestyle, Milly would fit in well. There was just something about her that made me think more aristocracy than Tennyson Crescent. Theo was still sore and needed some help getting to the car. He said he hadn't realised how ill he was and now he was feeling so much better.

'Well, my newfound freedom didn't last long and I still have another two years to finish my degree.'
'It will soon go,' I suggested, 'once you are back in the swing.'
'Yes, you are right. I will probably go on and do a Master's if I get a good grade.'
'Son, you will get a first. This is just a hiccup.'
'Sure thing, Tiger's Eyes,' Milly agreed. I glanced at my son's eyes in the daylight and realised, yes, they were a shade of pale brown tinged with green. Not really a tiger's colouring but close enough and that's how Milly saw them. Theo didn't protest at his nickname which surprised me. A lot about him had surprised me in the last few days. I almost didn't know him. Where was the barrier he erected around himself which I had felt unable to penetrate?

I couldn't wait to get home and settle Theo in.

A few days later, we had a telephone call for Milly. 'Who is it?' I asked. 'It's her mother Lady Marriot.' Well, she didn't sound too pleased this Lady Marriot. 'Milly,' I shouted, 'it's your mother.' A heated exchange took place for the next ten minutes. 'Well, I am sorry, Mummy. I will go back. I needed to be with Theo. No, please don't come and fetch me. You are embarrassing me now. Yes, I promise I will go back next week. Thank you, Mummy. I will see you soon. Give my love to Daddy, and please ask him not to be cross.'

'Sorry about that, Carrie. Mummy gets a bit heated at times.'

'Well, that is understandable, Milly. You have left your degree course, so she is quite rightly upset. By the way, I didn't realise your parents were titled.' Although I said this more to myself, I thought they would be somehow.

'Oh yes, Daddy was something in the city and was knighted some years ago for his services to a banking dynasty.'

'Tell me more,' I asked.

'I would if I could, Carrie, but I really don't know any more than that. I was an only child brought up by a nanny. My parents graced the London scene, and I was more of an inconvenience. They seemed at the time cold and unfeeling unlike the warmth which you and Charlie share.' 'So our laid-back, upside down, back to front lifestyle did have its compensations,' I thought to myself.

'I struggle at university, Carrie. Theo is so clever, and I love him to bits. I know he will leave me behind, but that's a risk I am prepared to take.'

'If things are meant to be, Milly, they will happen one way or the other. Just value the present and hope for the future.'

Well, we all fell in love with Milly. Phoebe thought she was fab. Jack said she was brill. Pat just said, 'Where did Theo find her? Under a park bench?' Secretly, I could tell, she was fond of Milly too.

As Theo recovered, his arrogance returned. 'Carrie, please stop fussing,' were his bywords. He would soften slightly when Milly appeared. He knew her background, and how lucky he had been! I never really know what was going on in his mind which was probably just as well. I was pleased he had what I could only term as a comfortable relationship with Milly.

'So where is this shack then?' Milly asked on Sunday morning. 'About three-quarters of an hour away,' Charles said. 'Can we go then?'
'Okay, let's load some tea, coffee, and food and be off.' Jack was first in the car; he was very excited about seeing Albert again.

The wind whistled around our ears as we unloaded the car. 'It is very bleak here,' Milly stated the obvious. 'That's why we like it,' I added, probably more sharply than I intended. 'Sorry,' Milly said, 'it wasn't a criticism. I meant it is somehow ethereal and what an interesting landscape! You are so lucky, Tiger's Eyes, to have spent your childhood here.' Theo looked thoughtful for a moment and really shocked me with his next statement. 'As Doctor Seuss once said, "You never know the value of a moment until it becomes a memory."' 'Wow,' I thought, 'that is the closest I am going to get to my son's real feelings about the shack.'

'Well, where 'ave u'um straggly lot been then? I missed yu'm all.'
'Albert, hello. Sorry, Theo was poorly, so we have been taking care of him.'
'Oose the lemon with legs in the corner?' Milly had a huge yellow sweater on with yellow leggings and black boots. 'This is Milly, Albert. Theo's friend.'
'Well, I won't be squeezing yur too hard then, 'cos you might spray juice everywhere.'
'Stop it, Albert. It's okay.' Milly laughed. We had forewarned her about Albert, so she half-knew what to expect.
'No fishing today then?'
'It's too rough even for me, missus. I just come down to check yur hut was okay and not blown away.' 'Well, I will put the kettle on, light the barbecue if we can find some dry wood and cook our food and get warm.'
We managed with Albert's help to get everything going. Wrapped up against the cold, we played I – spy and truth or dare and attempted a game of cricket. Theo sat wrapped up in a chair enjoying the

spectacle with more colour in his cheeks than I had seen for a long time. Milly said she wanted to stay here forever. 'Not possible, zesty lemon.' Theo smiled. 'Uni beckons and the bright lights of London for Christmas.'

I sensed the sadness in Milly's voice when she said, 'I know. I cannot offend Mummy and Daddy any more by staying away, and at least they have invited you. Well, they had before all this happened. I just hope they won't renege on their promise.'

'Thank you for today,' Milly said. 'I have loved it so much. Thank you for the net-mending lesson, Albert.' Jack was over the moon to bowl Albert out in cricket. 'That's one to me.' He licked his finger and drew the figure in the air. To be honest, Albert was glad to be out. His running days were well and truly over.

'We will see you soon, Albert. We just need to see Theo safely back to university.'

'Goodbye, Albert,' Theo said. I sensed a sadness in his voice. 'I have my seagull on my bedside table in my room. I treasure it.'

'I knoes you do, lad. I sees the look on yur face when I give it yur all them years ago.'

'Bye, Albert,' we shouted as he shuffled away up the hill.

I had a hint of sadness watching him. How much longer will he be coming here to fish, mend his nets, and amuse Jack and his friends? 'Stop it,' I told myself. 'He is probably a lot younger than he looks.' His weather-beaten face was probably down to years at sea in all weathers.

I took Milly to the museum where I worked and introduced her to Mr I Can . . . and Mary and Sheila. 'Oh, what a lovely place to work, Carrie! I would love to be doing something like this.'

'Well, who knows maybe you will one day?' It did cross my mind that probably not. If she and Theo stayed together, he would probably expect more of her. He had been rather scathing of my efforts here. 'For goodness sake, Carrie, you are much better than this!' he had exclaimed on a couple of occasions. I defended myself although why I don't know, telling him it was a job and it paid the bills.

Sheila wasn't too sure what to say to Milly, so just offered a tour of the museum. They were gone for ages, and I thanked Sheila when they came back and asked, 'What is outstanding that needs looking at?' A pile of papers landed on my desk with a thud. 'Just these,' she said. 'I will make some tea and we can go through them.' Milly sat patiently whilst I studied the notes, letters, and photographs, making up the wad of paperwork.

'I am so pleased to have met you, Milly,' I said as we drove Theo and her back to university for what was left of the term. 'I am going to work really hard,' she said. It had dawned on me we hadn't asked what subjects she was taking. We had been so concerned about Theo. 'What are you reading, Milly?' 'Oh, Art History, mainly the Pre Raphaelites.' 'How apt!' I thought. 'Do you know they were at Oxford and The Light of the World by Holman Hunt hangs in Keble College?' 'Yes I do.' I laughed. 'Good luck,' I said, but at the same time thought what use will this be to her in the years to come. Milly cut across my thoughts. 'Don't worry about Theo. He is in safe hands.' 'I am here,' Theo said, shifting from one foot to the other in exasperation. 'Welcome back, Theo.' I smiled to myself.

A voice of authority drifted across the campus, 'Miss Marriot, I would like a word with you.'

'Oh, Lordy, lordy, here goes,' Milly said under her breath. 'See you later, Theo.'

Standing in front of the bursar, her tutor, and somebody taking notes, Milly had half an hour of berating. Did she realise how privileged she was to have a place at Oxford? 'This is a warning. If this happens again, you will be sent down.' Milly knew in her heart of hearts, this would have been a lot worse if her father had been a random Joe Bloggs.

CHAPTER NINE
Carrie

Phoebe was lost without Theo to rub up the wrong way. She was teaching dance and drama at the local technical college, so at least, she had something to occupy her lively imagination. I think Jack was pleased with the peace and quiet. I missed the banter even if at times, it drove me to distraction. Phoebe was definitely a wind-up merchant where her brothers were concerned. She did have other things to keep her occupied now.

'They had all got two left feet,' she said in exasperation when she got home. 'Some I swear have five.'

'Stephen thinks he is Romeo, you know, the Shakespearian hero.' 'Well, I think I know that one, Phoebe. There are not too many boys named Romeo that I know of.' She ignored my remark and carried on. 'I don't like to tell him he has as much finesse as a sledge hammer. He thinks he can charm the birds from the trees, the feathered variety and the human variety. "Stephen, we need a word," that's what I told him, Carrie. It was water off a ducks back.'

'I am sure you will get through to him, Phoebe. He probably does it for effect knowing he is winding you up.'

'I have already got one of those at home,' she said, glaring at Jack. 'What have I done?' he said, a look of pure innocence on his face. 'Where do you want me to start?' Phoebe asked. 'Now, now, children, let's call a truce, shall we? And work out what we can do about Stephen.'

'I think a visit to the shack, and oh, whoops, we locked him in and forgot him!'

'Not a good idea, love. I am sure he is not that bad. Want a bet?'

'I'm off to get changed. I have an inspection early tonight to check my insurances are in place and up to date. Then a few of us are going to the pub. Don't wait up, Carrie.' Charles said he would. 'You may be eighteen, young lady, but you are still my daughter, and I want to know you are safe.'

Phoebe had kept her diaries from the time she could write. On one page, she had written, 'Phoebe loves Albert' in large letters. 'Well, we all loved Albert.'

'I love the shack too,' she had written. 'I hope we come here till we die.' Well, she hadn't reckoned on growing up and growing out of spending time with Carrie and Charlie and going her own independent way.

'Albert gave me a kite,' she remembered, 'and I loved it. I got the strings all tangled, but Charlie undid them for me. We played on the beach, and Theo built a house for crabs, but they didn't like it and one bit me. Charlie made it better. Charlie makes everything better I think. We have a barbecue today. Albert brought us fish to cook. I don't know if I like the smell but it tastes good. We do lots of things at the shack. We have nights there sometimes, and I love my snugly bunk. Carrie works in a museum and teaches me school work. Then I can play with my friends who live down the road. They go to a school, but I learn at home.'

Phoebe's friends Jacqueline and Anne were always at our house, which pleased me in a way because home schooling could be quite isolating. Not that Theo suffered too much; he welcomed the idea of being wrapped up in his own little world. It suited him fine to pick and choose his companions.

We took Phoebe and her friends to our seaside retreat on more than one occasion. We were good friends with both sets of parents. I had the feeling we were objects of ridicule sometimes. Both fathers flirted outrageously with me. Maybe I was a refreshing change to their tight-lipped wives. Sounds a bit harsh coming from me, but they are a bit strait-laced, which wasn't difficult in comparison to us. They eyed Charles with what seemed a cross between, 'what are you doing with her?' and 'are you for real?'

We brought their children back covered in sand, mud, and silt from our hunts on the beach for shells and driftwood. Jacqueline's parents said she couldn't come with us again. 'Oh, come on,' Charles said, 'don't be such a stick-in-the-mud, if you will pardon the pun.' 'We had fun, Mummy. Please let me go again.' 'We will see,' Mrs Tight Lip . . . said through gritted teeth. Anne's parents, who were well travelled and possibly more moneyed than the rest of us put together, looked at things differently. They felt Anne was learning from her trips with us and saw it more as an education. They knew I was an Oxford graduate and somehow trust came with my degree. Besides as she so condescendingly put it, 'I did have one extremely clever (if not altogether gifted with the social graces) son.'

We had been accepted into this tight-knit circle, so I said very little and just went with the flow.

Well, it was Christmas day, and we were off to the shack armed with a cooked turkey and vegetables wrapped in foil to keep warm. We took a trifle and cream and some cheeses with crackers. No, Theo, as I said before, he was with Milly. Phoebe was with friends, so we had Jack and Freddie to share our food. It was mild for this time of the year. One of those wet Yuletides which in a way was better for us. We couldn't come if we had snow and ice.

No sign of anyone except a couple of dog walkers. No Albert. He was probably at home with his family. It seemed odd not being a complete family, but times had moved on and things had changed. Pat had gone to one of her son's, and although she was not too happy about it, she decided to take up the invitation which she felt was offered more out of duty than really wanting her there.

'Don't be silly, Pat,' I tried to reassure her. 'I am sure they will love to have you,' I said, knowing full well, I probably agreed with her intuition.

We sat on the steps eating our lunch and intermittingly singing carols at the top of our voices. No one around to annoy. Freddie burst into song with 'Frostie the Snowman' and was really enjoying himself. I thought not for the first time how fate lends a hand in life. Just a chance meeting in a park and here he was growing up beside Jack and one of his best friends.

'This is Stephen, Carrie.' Phoebe made a show of introducing him, her arms remonstrating as always. It was Boxing Day, and Phoebe said she would like to spend it with us. We hadn't reckoned on a visitor as well.

I looked at this long, lanky, thin youth in front of me and thought clumsiness did come in some strange packages. 'Hello, Stephen. I'm Carrie. How do you do?' 'Very well, thank you, er . . . um Carrie.' 'Hi, I'm Charlie.' Charles came out of nowhere hearing voices. 'Well, I can see where you get your looks from,' Stephen said to Phoebe, glancing from Charles to Phoebe and back again. Stephen looked very awkward, so I quickly changed the subject. 'It is nice to meet you, Stephen, and a belated Happy Christmas.'

'What made you join Phoebe's class, Stephen?' I addressed him looking up to what was quite a handsome face. Floppy blond hair covered his eyes, which I could just about see. 'I like drama,' he answered honestly. 'It takes me to another level outside myself.' 'Oh really?' I said, not too sure what that meant.

'My parents want me to be an accountant, solicitor, or someone with a proper job. I just want to be an actor/dancer or anything that comes with a theatre and stage. Besides which I cannot get to grips with sitting down for hours on end and on top of that looking at figures and training manuals all day long.'

'Well, you have a good tutor in Phoebe.' I smiled. 'One or two of her protégés have gone on to greater things.'

'Well, I am not that ambitious. Just need to earn a living before I am thrown out in to the big wide world.'

'You just need to listen and take on board Phoebe's ideas and suggestions. If it doesn't work for you, Stephen, then it's off to a class for budding accountants.' 'Oh no,' he shuddered.

We sat down for supper. I had to say Stephen was quite flexible. He had to fold almost double to sit at our small table. 'Maybe a job in a circus as the "Incredible Bendy Accountant" beckons.' 'What are you smiling at, Carrie?' 'Nothing, Phoebe. Just had a thought. That's all.'

'You are wicked, Carrie,' Charles said when I told him through fits of giggles what was going through my mind.

Well, Stephen had his looks but quite where he was going to take them from here I had no idea. 'Phebes sure has her work cut out,' Jack butted in. 'You were not supposed to hear that, Jack,' I said, giving him a pretend clip around the ear. 'Oh whoops!' he said. 'Sorry, but you were speaking rather loudly. It's a good job they have gone. Otherwise, you would be in trouble, Carrie.'

'Thank you, Jack. I think I know that.'

'What did you think of Stephen?' Phoebe was addressing Charles and me. 'Well, I don't really know at this precise moment,' Charles, ever protective of his little girl, was at a loss for words. 'What have we done to our children, Carrie? They seem to attract odd characters.' 'That is mean, Charlie,' Phoebe said, 'and unfair. He is proving to be a difficult student, but he is very nice, and I am sure we will get somewhere eventually.' 'Oh, I do hope not,' Charles muttered under his breath, probably thinking 'we might get somewhere' meant more than his theatre work.

The following year, an envelope dropped through our letter box. I knew what it was before I opened it. Theo had said he could have two guest tickets for his graduation. I cannot believe how quickly the time had gone by. My mind drifted back to my graduation and how a very old and infirm Aunt Maude had made a huge effort to attend. We would be there for our son, and how proud we both would be!

CHAPTER TEN
Carrie

Charles and I sat side by side waiting for the ceremony to begin. As I had said before, I know the procedure. Charles shifted uncomfortably in his seat. This was a double whammy for us: Theo's graduation and his foray into the big wide world. I hadn't realised it would be such a big wide world. He had called to say he had been offered a sabbatical in a pharmaceutical company in the States doing scientific work on a new drug. 'Carrie, it's not forever,' he had said over the silence that followed his announcement. 'I know, Theo. I am so very proud of you.' Secretly, I gave myself an imaginary pat on mine and Charles's backs. We had between us got a son to be extremely proud of.

I was going to miss him so much. I would add I am extremely proud of all three of my children, but it was Theo's time at that moment.

We sat through the procession of dignitaries, honorary doctorates to the deserving, some more deserving than others, and then the speeches. I glanced around the expectant faces of the graduates and had a feeling of pride for every single one of them.

I picked out Amelia's parents, Lord and Lady Marriot, quite easily. She was the only one wearing a hat. We had never met but had spoken on the phone about Theo and Milly's friendship. There were differing opinions about this, and we clashed somewhat, so our contact was very little. My son had achieved a first-class honours degree in Biomedical Sciences. Milly got a third in Art History. However, it didn't stop the Marriots from looking down on us with some consternation.

'Theo Jones, First Class with Honours The Sciences.' I thought my heart would burst out of my chest when he was called to receive his degree. Charles looked very pale and completely mesmerised by the whole of academia. We had a long way to go with the ceremony. Theo was near the front of the alphabet. By the time we reached the Y's, Charles had nodded off. I nudged him with my elbow just hoping he wasn't going to start snoring.

As we got up to go and congratulate Theo for the umpteenth time, a voice boomed in my ear. 'Well, if it isn't Caroline Connaught that was?' 'It still is,' I said as I stared into a face that looked like a ripe tomato that had been thrown against a wall. 'I guess you are here for the fruit of your loins,' he bellowed. I gazed from the flat face to the little woman by his side clutching her handbag as if her life depended on it, the cogs whirring in my brain trying to place this buffoon. 'This is Deirdre, and who might this be?' he said, nudging Charles with such brute force it nearly knocked him sideways. 'I am Charlie, and if you will excuse us, we need to go and find our son.' 'Well, Charlie, pleased to meet you.' 'Come on,' Deidre said very quietly, almost indiscernibly, 'we must catch up with Miriam.' I guess she was extremely embarrassed and not for the first time, although I did sense a look of idol worship in her eyes for this oaf.

'Who on earth . . . Don't go there. Charles, I have no idea.' Then the cogs stopped turning, and it all came back to me. It was Gerald from my uni days, known as my 'fumble partner' you know – the boy you try to get it on with, but it never quite works. The years had not been kind to Gerro as he was known amongst his friends. How could Mother Nature do this to one human being! The sandy-haired boy I knew bore no resemblance whatsoever to the ebullient (and that's a polite term) man we had just been accosted by.

I left it at 'don't go there' as far as Charles was concerned. I couldn't bear a Spanish inquisition. Well, that wouldn't happen, but I knew I would get twenty questions or possibly forty, who knows?

We congregated outside for any photo opportunities and introduced ourselves to Amelia's parents. 'Your son did good.' Lord Marriot guffawed in that annoying upper-middle-class way. Lady Marriot breathed in and exhaled in a sniffy kind of way and grudgingly agreed. 'Of course, it was Theo's fault Milly didn't do well, putting her off her studies and generally being a bad influence.' 'Oh really, is that so?' Charles said. 'Well, she did abscond when Theo went in to hospital.'

'That was two years ago,' I said. I could see this was going nowhere, and then finally, to put the mockers on the whole proceedings, Milly announced, 'You do know I am off to New York with Theo, don't you, Mummy and Daddy?' I thought Lady Marriot was going to expire on the spot. Her very large hat once worn at a jaunty angle now fell over her face. 'Over my dead body,' she said. 'Quite possibly, Mummy,' Milly muttered. 'Let the two young things have their head, Felicity.' Lord Marriot guffawed again. Theo had that 'get me away from here' look on his face. 'Oh really, Nigel, when are you ever on my side?' I intervened saying, 'It isn't a case of sides. We have two young people here who want to be together,' fleetingly remembering Charles and my early days. 'And please realise they are both stood here and it is their decision,' probably said more sharply than I intended.

'What's the tie, old man?' Lord Marriot asked Charles, changing the subject. I could tell Charles had absolutely no idea what he was talking about. He owned one tie which had been washed and pressed so many times it shone like a Belisha beacon. 'Oh,' I said, 'it's "The Ancient order of Pickle and Chutney Makers." What's yours?' 'Old Harrovian, my dear,' he said in his superior voice. 'Of course, it is,' I replied. I could tell he was still trying to work out what the ancient order of pickle and chutney was.

Lord Marriot obviously full of copious amounts of pre-ceremony tipple and probably had a hip flask as well didn't get my joke. Although judging by Lady Marriot's expression, she did.

Theo had related sometime ago his experience spending time with Milly at her parents' home. 'If I didn't like her so much, Carrie, I would have left. They treat their staff well, but there is still the them and us scenario which I found uncomfortable.' 'Different backgrounds, different priorities,' I said at the time to my son.

'Yes, I know,' he said, 'but Milly is different. We have helped each other stay on the straight and narrow through our studies. I owe her a lot. She understands me, and I get where she is coming from.'

I thought of Charles and me again. Theo must have read my thoughts because he said, 'Just like you and Charlie, Carrie.'

'I understand you have a shed on the beach somewhere,' Lady Marriot said over the general furore going on around us, parents trying to vie for their offspring's attention with cameras clicking everywhere. 'Do smile, Jemima!' 'Oh, Frederick, surely you don't have to be so rude!' 'Penelope, you have a first. Please allow us to be proud of you.' 'Well, there is proud and then there is pride. I do not want the life squeezed out of me and to be eaten alive by copious kisses, you are embarrassing me!'

'Yes, we do,' Charles said. 'It isn't exactly ours. We adopted it several years ago as no one seemed to own it, and it is a bit more than a shed. It's a holiday shack.' 'Well, there isn't a lot of difference!' 'Look,' I said, 'this is Milly and Theo's day. Let's concentrate on them and their achievements.' 'Quite right,' Charles said in a grateful, 'Thank you, Carrie' voice.

I could tell Theo had had enough. 'Thank you for coming, Carrie and Charlie. We are meeting up with some of our peers if you would like to join us for drinks at our local.' Well, their local was where Charles and I met and where we spent time whilst Theo was in hospital. 'Bitter sweet memories,' I thought. 'We will just hand in our gowns and mortar boards and be with you,' Milly said in a hurried tone. 'Come on, Tiger's Eyes, let's get rid of these.'

'We have our chauffeur on standby,' Lord Marriot shouted as if he wanted everyone in the vicinity to hear. 'He can take us to wherever this pub is.' 'We are okay. Thank you,' Charles said politely. 'We will follow in our own car.' 'I will come with you,' Theo said, secretly squeezing my hand. We parked in St Giles and walked along to the pub, arm in arm with our son. 'Milly has had a dreadful time,' Theo said. 'It's amazing how someone who looks to have it all has nothing.' Lord and Lady Marriot stood outside the pub garden, leaving their chauffeur quietly idling the car wondering where he could park and wait. We directed him back to where we had parked. 'An hour will be fine,' Lady M shouted to her driver. 'Okay, Ma 'am.' He nodded as he drove off. Theo and Milly hugged each other as if they had been apart for weeks rather than maybe half an hour. I loved my son with my whole being and was so pleased he and Milly found each other. She was so right for him and our family.

Felicity (as we are allowed to call Lady Marriot now) hadn't got large ears, but they were the only thing stopping her flying saucer of a hat from falling any further down over her face. She looked like the morning after the night before. I am glad I kept my outfit simple. I didn't have too much choice lacking in funds as we do. Both Theo and Charles had said I looked really nice, as I have said before nice would do.

'Okay, whose for drinky poos,' said an already inebriated Nigel aka Lord Marriot. 'Thank you,' I said. 'I will have half of lager.' 'Pint for me please,' said Charles. Theo and Milly settled for a beer each too.

In the early autumn sunshine, we could have been any family sat here in the garden, but, you could cut the atmosphere with a knife, two families colliding like two crossing tides. We had been joined by a few others, but Felicity was determined to have centre stage.

'About this American thing,' she said in her pedantic tone. 'What about it?' Theo asked. 'Well, why are you taking my daughter away from us?' 'Milly has a mind of her own,' Theo said through his teeth. 'Too right, Tiger's Eyes,' Milly said in agreement. 'She wants to come, and I want her there. I am lucky enough to have parents who always encourage me to be my own person and follow my chosen path.' 'Really?' said Felicity, crossing and uncrossing her legs and getting her heel stuck in the grass tutting as she parted her shoe from her foot to disengage the heel for about the fourth time. I made a mental note never to cross the path of these people again. Unless Theo and Milly married, which I hoped if they did, it was years away I would not need to see them again.

Felicity obviously thought differently. 'You must weekend with us soon,' she said air-kissing both cheeks as we said goodbye. 'I cannot promise anything at the moment,' I said in what I hoped sounded like a regretful tone. 'Work is busy for both of us, and I have two others at home to look after.' Charles looked relieved but said we will keep in touch, which prompted a prod from me. He was far too polite for his own good.

'We will be home in a couple of days,' Theo said. I got a hug, which surprised me. I think he knew how I felt and wanted to reassure me. 'Can we go to the shack?' Milly asked. 'I would love to spend some time there.' Felicity looked as if a bad smell had developed under her nose. 'Really,' she said, 'how Neanderthal!' 'Mummy, Really?' Milly said exasperated, 'So sorry, Carrie and Charlie.' 'Don't apologise,' Charles said. 'We are used to it. Remind me to tell you the story about Freddie.' Whilst Nigel was struggling to stay upright and Felicity looked as if she was disappearing under a cloud of tulle, Charles put his arm around my waist, his hand dropped down to stroke my bottom which he hoped would infuriate the life out of Lady Marriot. Public displays of affection were probably not her scene, and her pinched mouth confirmed just that.

'I love you, Carrie,' Milly whispered in my ear as we said our goodbyes. 'See you soon. I love you too,' I mouthed. This bundle of red untamed hair and colourful clothes had won my son's heart and that was good enough for me. I think Charles remained neutral, although I knew he liked Milly very much. I wondered what kind of life she had had with these parents of hers. I don't like to ask too many questions, but I could guess it wasn't too good. She had mentioned before that there was no time in their busy schedule for her. It saddened me and made me even more aware of her vulnerability.

I wondered not for the first time today what Albert would make of Lord and Lady Marriot. Not a lot if I read him correctly. I think they would get their life history in one fell swoop!

CHAPTER ELEVEN
Carrie

'Hi, we are back,' I called as we got in the door. Phoebe was watching the television, something she rarely did. 'Where is Jack?' I asked. 'Round at Pat's. Trying to interest her in a game of Monopoly.'

'I hope he isn't tiring her out.'

'I don't think so, Carrie. She came to ask him if he wanted to play a board game. I declined as I have a class in a minute. I must go soon. How did it go? How is my long-lost brother?' I regaled her with stories of Lord and Lady Marriot which had her crying with laughter. I told her about the ceremony and how dignified it all was but omitted the undignified Gerald. 'Theo and Milly are coming home at the weekend, so we will probably go to the shack. Milly asked if we can take her.' 'Great,' said Phoebe. 'We can see Albert, and Theo can give him his carving.'

'I forgot about that,' I thought. I hope it was okay. It had been in the shack awhile. I suppose I could have given it to him, but I thought as it was Theo's gift, he would like to hand it over himself. I must get out of these clothes and shoes. My feet were sore, and I longed to be comfortable. 'Oh goody,' said Charles, rubbing his hands together. 'For goodness sake!' Phoebe laughed. 'You two, I don't know!'

'How is Stephen?'

'Oh, you know mesmerised by the Jones family. He will probably come to the shack with us next time.'

'Do you really think so, Phoebe. He doesn't seem the type to muck in.'

'Well, we take a bit of getting used to, Carrie, but I wouldn't have it any other way. We come as a package. Take us or leave us I say.' She kissed the top of my head on her way out.

Phoebe said her classes were going really well. She was hoping to expand and take her undoubted talent to other towns and villages around us. We were proud of her too. She had her own little car having passed her test the second time, so she could take her business wherever she thought fit. The only criticism from her driving examiner was her speeding. She told me he had said, 'You need to slow down, Phoebe.' She thought the faster she went, the quicker she would pass her test. I said, 'It doesn't work like that.' 'I know, Carrie, just teasing. I just wanted to get rid of my L plates and start saving some money.'

'Well, it hasn't cost you too much,' I re-iterated. Charles did most of the teaching, him of the endless patience, I know, but I paid for some lessons. Phoebe melted my heart with her big blue eyes.

Theo and Milly arrived in flurry of bags and books. 'Hi, everyone,' Milly shouted from the driveway. 'I couldn't wait to get here. Theo is in one of his reclusive moods, and I need someone to talk to.'

'Hi, son. Are you okay?' I asked casually. 'Don't fuss, Carrie.' Where have I heard that before?

'Well, you can talk to me, Milly.'

'I am so sorry about my parents,' she said in a rush of apologies. 'Please don't worry about it, Milly. I am sure they have your best interests at heart. They just don't show it.'

'Don't you believe it. Mother is still going on about me not staying at home. I have tried to point out there is no reason to be a bird in a gilded cage, which is how I would feel. No job I did would be suitable in their eyes. I hope to find something in the States to occupy me, even if it is just in a diner. The waiters go around on rollerblades you know? What fun that would be!' 'Great, if you want your food in your lap,' Theo said rather sarcastically. 'Oh come on, Tiger's Eyes. Don't take me too seriously.' I didn't question my son any further. 'Where's Charlie?' Theo asked lazily from the depths of the sofa. Well, very deep actually as most of the springs had gone, although he didn't seem to notice. 'Down the pub I think with his workmates. We didn't think you were arriving till tomorrow. It is so good to see you. I would like to ask about your new work,' I said tentatively. I didn't want my head bitten off. 'Tomorrow, Carrie. I am tired after the journey, and I need to unload some stuff. Am I in with Jack?' 'Yes, he is so looking forward to having you home for a while.'

'Well, he can do me the honour of not talking his way through the night like he usually does.' 'Welcome home, Theo, in more ways than one,' I muttered under my breath.

We were to have two weeks with Theo and Milly. Well, Theo, for that time and Milly for part of it. She needed to go home to Scotswood House to unpack her university books and work and pack for the States. Theo said he couldn't face her mother again, beside which he didn't want the third degree about his intentions regarding Milly, so Charlie offered to drive her. 'Ooh, I get to spend time with the most handsome man in the world!' she giggled. I said, 'I wasn't going.' Theo said, 'Good lord!' He showed some humour. I felt I needed to bow and kiss his feet. Well, not quite, but nearly. 'Thank you, Charlie, very much.' 'Well, if you behave, I might come back for you,' he said, 'if your mother doesn't eat me alive the first time around. And please, I hope that soppy hat is consigned to hat heaven. Did she know it didn't suit her?' 'Stop it, Charles,' I admonished. 'It has probably bred with the brown one she has just like it, and we will be met by lots of brown and blue things bobbing about on legs in the drive.' Milly put her hands up and crooked her fingers in a mock-horror movie way. 'Well, I am supposed to have an aura of class so I am told. However, I think my halo has dropped down over my head like your mother's net and tulle creation.' 'Whatever happens, Milly, they are your parents. Try to be patient,' I said, trying to save the day. 'I know,' said Milly, wanting to be magnanimous about it all. 'It's just that I don't have very happy memories of being young. I was left constantly with nannies whilst Mummy and Daddy mixed with the hoi poloi. Mummy had soirees with her cronies, and Daddy organised shooting parties which I hated. What was the point of breeding pheasants and grouse just to release them in to the sky to be shot at by overweight, much moneyed, grunting marksmen and women paying huge amounts for the privilege? Thank goodness, they didn't join the hunting set. That would be worse with the horses and hounds galloping across our grounds chasing a creature who didn't stand a chance. Even Mummy drew the line at that. Daddy looked ridiculous on a horse and Mummy can't ride.' A caricature of Felicity on a pony, in her high heels and her hat down over her eyes hovered into my mind. 'It is not funny,' Milly said in exasperation as I smiled inwardly. 'Sorry, Milly. I just had a picture in my mind of Lord and Lady Marriot trying to ride out with the hunt,' I said, lying slightly.

'Well let's face it, Milly. You are experiencing life at both ends of the social spectrum.' 'Hmm, and I know which one I prefer,' she answered. Any more tea in that pot please?'

'Do you fancy coming to class with me one day?' Phoebe asked Milly. 'I just know you can dance. You have that elegant way about you.' I smiled to myself. Green and pink ankle-length skirt, blue and black socks, and a jumper somewhere in between, pretty and hippy, but I didn't think elegance came in to it. 'That okay with you, Tiger's Eyes?' 'Anything for a bit of peace and quiet,' Theo sighed. 'Chess for us then, son, okay?' I had taught Charles to play chess during the long nights in our bedsit. Now, he was better than me, not a grand master but very good.

The feel good factor I think you call it, Jack was next door at Pat's again with Freddie. I sat reading my latest Mills and Boon whilst my two men played chess. I know, I know, but it was all I could concentrate on at the moment. I had a house full, a job, and a shack to maintain. They were not my favourite read, but this was it for the moment. When I get more time, I would explore George Orwell's *Animal Farm* or J. D. Salinger's *Catcher in the Rye*, and I might even dip in to a Stephen Hawking. Who am I kidding, what is wrong with a bit of romance, eh? Besides which I was about to lose my son to some research project on the other side of the Atlantic. That thought filled most of my mind all the time.

'Checkmate,' my son said not for the first time. 'You are losing your touch Charlie old man,' he said to Charlie. 'Less of the old, thank you. I can cope with losing but old? No.'

'So how did it go?' I asked Phoebe and Milly as they came tumbling through the door. 'Fab,' said Milly. 'And have you seen Stephen? phwoar is all I can say.' Theo appeared nonplussed at first about the whole thing. 'I don't do competition,' he said in the lazy way he speaks when bored. 'Oh, no competition,' Milly chirruped. 'Stephen wins hands down.' 'You have done it now, my girl.' Theo all of a sudden came to life. He picked Milly up, threw her over his shoulder, went outside, and deposited her in our not too clean garden pond. Fortunately, there was no fish, just green slime and weed. Pat came out hotly followed by Jack and Freddie to see what all the fuss was about.

'Don't worry, Pat. Just teaching this girl a lesson.' Jack thought he was serious for a moment and then realised his brother may be many things but he wouldn't harm a fly. Besides which Milly was laughing, so it was all in good fun.

Theo helped Milly out of the water saying, 'Welcome to the Theo Jones initiation ceremony that comes with infidelity.' They collapsed together in a heap on the soggy grass where the grimy water had made its way over the edge of the pond. Through the murk, Milly was laughing and protesting her innocence. 'Too late now, Amelia, but you will think twice before you mention Stephen again.'

'Did I hear a yes?'

'Yes, yes, yes,' Milly shouted at the top of her voice.

It was odd to see Theo this way. As we know, he was a complex character with a myriad of personalities which most of the time I found hard to keep up with. Milly seemed to bring out the best in him.

Milly and Theo had baths and changed their clothes whilst I made soup for us all. Pat was anxious to hold on to Jack and Freddie, so they stayed with her for their supper.

'We will leave you in peace, Pat,' Jack said, realising she looked very tired. He and Freddie enjoyed their time with her, but Carrie had warned them not to stay too long and tire her out. 'Supper was great. Thank you. See you soon.' 'Bye, lads,' Pat said. She felt sad as they left but also was overcome with weariness.

Freddie spent a lot of time with us. His father had recovered well but was only allowed to work part-time on doctor's orders. His mother was now working too, their middle-class lifestyle out the window. I tutor Freddie to help with his Maths, and I had to say his parents had thanked me on a number of occasions. Things were so different now. Freddie had grown into a polite and likeable young man and was Jack's best friend. Who would have thought the meeting in the park all those years ago would have such a satisfactory ending? His parents were still quite offhand about our shack and asked a lot of questions, mainly about what we do whilst there, and what do we cook with and so on?

I had explained about our walks and the barbecue. Freddie had already told them about his time with us, but somehow it wasn't enough, and they sometimes didn't want to let the subject go. All that really mattered to me was keeping Jack and Freddie occupied and happy.

We cannot please everyone. We found that out a long time ago. Justifying ourselves had long been sidelined as it was no longer an option. 'We are who we are, and that's the way it stays!'

'Oh no!' Theo exclaimed as Albert came wandering along the beach. 'You still around then?' 'Well if it ain't Brain o' Britain condescending to pay um a visit.' After the friendly hugs, Albert asked, "ow did that there thing go where you gets wot u 'u'um worked 'ard to get?' Theo regaled the experience only lightly touching on Lord and Lady Marriot's input. I smiled as Milly sidled up to Albert and gave him a quick kiss on the cheek. 'Away, wi' yum Lemon on legs,' he chuckled. 'Really, Albert, I am a graduate now. Please treat me with more respect!' 'Yur come to the wrong place for tha', lass,' Albert grunted. 'Wanna know more about net mending? I got some wot needs doing.' Milly knew she probably wouldn't see Albert again and wanted to spend as much time as possible with him. 'Is it okay, Carrie, if I go with Albert for a while.' 'Of course, it is. Oh, by the way, Theo, you have something for Albert in the shack.' 'Indeed I do. Just a minute, you old reprobate.' Theo found the carved boat he had made a couple of years earlier and presented it with a flourish. It was buried beneath some very damp library books which have long since passed the due return date. Dickens', *The Tale of two Cities*, that was us and the Marriots then, Theo fleetingly thought. 'It's a far, far better thing that I do, to rescue Milly from their clutches. Not very poetic but true.'

We had never seen Albert cry. Those blue eyes of his filled with tears as he gazed at his present. 'I got summat in me eye,' Albert said as he wiped at his face with a piece of old rag he found in his pocket. 'Thank you, boy, we bofe got fings now to remind um o' these times, lad.'

'Yous a coming, lemon on legs then.' Milly clutched Albert's arm and shouted, 'Lead on Macbeth,' in her best stoical voice. The comment was lost on Albert. 'Ooh the 'ells Macbeth when e's at 'ome?' 'Never mind.' Milly laughed. She turned as she went, looking at Carrie, Charles, Theo, and Jack sitting on the steps of the shack waving away and not for the first time realised how lucky she was to have them all, excited about the prospect of life with Theo in the States. 'Hang on,' Jack shouted, 'I'm coming with you.' 'C'mon me, lad, then,' Albert called. 'Get them there legs movin' we got work to do.'

'Right, who's for a walk?' Carrie asked Charles and Theo. They wandered off down the beach taking in the bleak landscape filled with a grey and a pale pink light which somehow reflected off the sea to form shadows as they went. 'I am going to miss this place,' Theo said completely out of the blue. 'Really,' Charles said, 'you surprise me son. I never really thought our time here suited you much.' 'I have to admit it didn't really, but as I said before, "You never know the value of a moment until it becomes a memory"' Quite a profound comment from my son, although as we know he copied it from someone else.

We collected driftwood to light our barbecue, which I had to say really was not much use now. We have scrubbed the grill so at least it was clean. We brought some beef burgers, potatoes, and some soup to cook on our primus. Crusty rolls and cake.

'Right, race you back,' Theo shouted. 'Oh that's not fair,' I said. 'You and Charles have longer legs than me.' 'Rubbish, we are carrying the wood, Carrie. Don't be such a spoil sport!'

Charles grabbed me by the wrist, and I half ran and was half tugged back. We all three fell in a breathless heap on the sand by the steps to our shack.

Albert brought Milly and Jack back just as Charles was having a good swear at the heap of tin which was our makeshift barbecue. 'I forgot the matches. Anyone got two boy scouts to rub together?' 'Very funny, Charlie,' Theo said with a hint of sarcasm. 'Well, just as well I smokes me pipe then ain't it, 'ere you are.' Albert handed over his matches, and with a lot of luck and a following wind (quite literally), the wood burst in to life.

'We've been singing shanties,' Jack said. 'Oh please not.' 'What shall we do with a drunken sailor?' 'I had heard that so many times from Charles when I started work in the maritime museum.'

'Well, that be the only one I knows,' Albert said, 'that an' a bit of *"O'er the sea to Skye"* which ain't exactly a shanty, though it be about a boat of sorts.'

'Come on,' Milly grabbed Theo's arm. 'Oh, I don't think so. The horn pipe is not my thing.' Milly grabbed Jack who in turn grabbed Charles and me to form a circle. Albert was not going to move from his comfy seat on one of our foldaway chairs.

We danced around like lunatics and sang out of tune. Theo decided to have his chef's hat on, that's a first I might add and keep Albert company.

Way-hay and up she rises
Way-hay and up she rises
Way – hay and up she rises
Early in the . . .

'You have to be kidding me!' Milly pulled up with a jerk which nearly sent us all flying.

'Please tell me this is one of those things you see in the desert when you are hot and tired, hungry and thirsty' 'A mirage,' I said. 'Yes, that's it. Please tell me those two people heading towards us are a mirage!'

Well, a mirage, they definitely are not; a very odd sight, they definitely are.

Lord Marriot in his tweeds and a deerstalker hat, Lady Marriot also head to toe in tweeds and a hat with a ridiculous feather sticking out of it. 'Oh Pllllease,' sighed Theo. 'Oh shit,' said Charles. 'Oh, oh, I don't know. Any old oh will do.' Jack dissolved in to fits of giggles. 'Shut up, darling,' I hissed, 'this is no laughing matter.'

Lord Marriot was the first one to speak. 'Your neighbour told us where to find you.' I made a mental note to clip Pat around the ear when I saw her, well an earbashing of some sort.

'Good heavens, what a surprise!' I said in my best English tones. Milly was struck dumb for the first time since we met her. Jack had disappeared inside the shack, and Albert was speechless, but not for long! Theo carried on cooking our supper trying to pretend they were not here.

'Ooo might u'um be then,' Albert said eventually in his best fisherman's drawl, probably knowing only too well who they are. 'This is Mummy and Daddy,' Milly said before they could answer. 'Be that right,' Albert said, amusement showing in his normally tired eyes. 'Lord and Lady Marriot, Nigel and Felicity,' Lord M shouted above the wind blowing in from the sea.

'Bloody cold in these parts,' Nigel said. 'What on earth makes you want to spend time around and old tin barrel and a wooden shed?' In my heart, I knew they wouldn't understand, so as I was about to say, 'Because we love it here,' Milly said, 'Don't be so rude, Daddy. We all love it here.' Lord M harrumphed what sounded like a, 'sorry but could have been anything.'

'Way- hay and up she rises,' Albert started singing and trying to puff on his pipe at the same time.

Felicity dissolved into fits of coughing as the smoke came her way. 'Sorry, missus. U'um need to be up wind outa me way.' 'Really?' Felicity sneezed, waving her hands in front of her face, being more dramatic than was necessary.

'Right, food is ready,' Theo announced. 'Carrie, have you got the plates out.' 'I have, son.' 'Will you be wanting any,' he asked Milly's parents. The first time he had acknowledged they were here. 'Oh, good lord, no thank you,' said Felicity in that 'I would rather walk a mile in concrete boots' tone of hers.

It must be obvious to any onlooker that the Marriots couldn't relate to our family and their devil may care attitude and the bone china crockery and beautiful marquetry tray used to serve the food. The wooden foldup table was bending under the weight of everything.

'U'um be any good at net mending,' Albert said to Nigel through mouthfuls of burger and potato as the bobble on his hat, no doubt knitted by the missus, took on a life of its own. 'I don't think so, old man,' Lord M guffawed again. 'I not be that old,' Albert said, a cloud passing over his bright blue eyes. 'It's a metaphor, not an insult, Albie.' 'It's Albert, and I don't know what u'um means.' 'Don't think about it, Albert. It's not worth worrying about,' Charles butted in to save the day.

'Well, we have brought you some things for your American trip,' Felicity said through chattering teeth to her daughter. 'I was coming home to pack my things, Mummy. Charlie was bringing me.' 'Oh well, never mind, darling. We have got most of your clothes. You didn't leave a lot behind, and besides which we are off to South of France with the Anstruthers next week, so thought it best to make sure you have everything you need.' 'You cannot stand, Arthur Anstruther, Mummy.' 'I know, darling, but needs must when you get a free holiday and sunshine to boot.' 'Well, I hope the sun shines for you, Mummy, because it doesn't always and October can be quite chilly there, so take some warm clothes.' Felicity looked quite taken aback. 'Really, how would you know Amelia?' 'Because, when Carrie met Charlie just after she'd graduated, her house mates had gone to St Tropez. Carrie couldn't go, and when they got back, they all said how much colder it was than they had anticipated.' Carrie had told the story to Milly one evening when she had asked how she and Charlie had met.

'What do you all do here for your ablutions?' Felicity piped up. 'We boil water to wash, and we use the toilet block built for the fishermen in exchange for keeping them clean. Cleaning doesn't take long because apart from Albert, there was only a couple of other trawler men, and they don't come too often now.'

'Well, it will be a change of scene if nothing else,' Felicity said, suddenly raising the South of France topic again.

The Marriots looked uncomfortable, so Carrie suggested we went back to their car with them and loaded Milly's things in to theirs.

'Don't worry, Carrie,' Theo offered. 'I will do it.' 'Me too,' Milly said. 'Well, goodbye er' Charlie, Carrie, and oh yes, Albert.' Jack hadn't appeared but hearing the word goodbye came through the door to wish them well, trying really hard not to laugh again.

'Farewell all,' Nigel blustered. 'Good riddance,' Albert said under his breath as they turned to walk away, his bobble still wobbling in the wind. At least Felicity's hat sat squarely on her head this time helped, no doubt by the decorative hat pin.

Milly hugged her parents and they shook hands with Theo. 'Look after our girl,' they said. 'I will,' Theo said, and under his breath, 'a lot better than you have.' 'I will write when I get to America,' Milly said as they drove away. Theo hugged Milly and asked, 'Will you miss them too much?' 'Probably a bit, but I have you, Tiger's Eyes'. 'How about you? I am sure you will miss Carrie and Charlie and your brother and sister.' 'I will very much. One of Carrie's sayings is, you give your children wings to fly and a nest to come home to. I know I . . . we will always have somewhere to return to if things don't go well or we get homesick.'

'Well, I have been saved a trip to the Marriots stately pile anyway,' Charles said with some relief. 'I wasn't really looking forward to it, so a big let off for me.' 'I expect Milly feels the same,' I added. 'Maybe she was worried about it too not knowing quite what sort of reception you would get.' 'Well, whatever we think, they are her parents, and I am sure she is sad to be leaving them.' 'Well, she chose to spend her last weeks in the UK with us, so that must tell you something, Carrie.'

'Well, I suppose it does, but I think it is more to do with being with Theo.' 'Yes, I suppose you are right, but it's great to have them both here.'

'Well, I best be off,' Albert got up rather stiffly. 'The missus will be a wondering where I is. Thank e for tea.' 'You are very welcome,' I said. 'We will be back soon.'

'We are going to miss you, Albert,' Theo and Milly gave him a hug. 'You take care, and I will see you when we get back next year.' 'You take care o' urselfs, I spect I get news 'of e from Carrie and Charlie.'

I felt a sudden loss of all that was precious to me. Then I thought, 'We are still here with Phoebe, Jack, and possibly Stephen and life moves on.' The only consistent thing in life is its inconsistency.

'Bye, Albert. See you soon,' I called after him knowing his eyes would be shadowed with sadness.

We doused the tin barrel, washed up, and stacked our things in the shack ready to head home.

CHAPTER TWELVE
Carrie

'I have a bone to pick with you, Patricia,' I said in my best school mistress voice, after we had unloaded the car. 'Oh don't,' Pat said.

'Who the hell are they? No, don't answer that. Come and have a cuppa and you can tell me all about what happened when they turned up at the shack? I am sorry, but they were very insistent and wouldn't go away till I told them where you were.'

If it was possible for two grown women to giggle for England, that was us. 'Albert asked if Lord Marriot was any good at net mending. Milly thought they were a mirage. Charles swore, and Jack disappeared inside the shack. Theo said nothing and just concentrated on his cooking. I just smiled sweetly and said, "Oh no or oh something." They eyed our food as if it was only fit for a dog's dinner. When I offered them some, you would think I had said, "Here you are. Have a sip from a poison chalice." Anyway just as well Albert wasn't exposing the insides of a mackerel with its head chopped off.'

'Talking of Albert, is he okay?'

'I think so, just sad to say goodbye to Theo and Milly.'

'Hello, everyone.' Phoebe came flying through the door almost literally having tripped over Milly's suitcase.

'Did you all have a good time? Okay what's funny?' I related the Lord and Lady Marriot's saga. 'You are kidding me, really? Where is the young lady?'

'Oh, she and Theo are sorting out their things for New York. Well, they have another week.'

'I know, but maybe it's a euphemism for we would like time to ourselves.'

'Well, I've got news of sorts, Carrie dearest. That very fine education you gave me has reaped rewards. I have an offer to set up my own dance and theatre group.' ('Please don't tell me you are moving away too.') 'Are you listening, Carrie?' 'Sorry, yes.' 'Well, there are grants available for which I am eligible, so I am looking at renting a small studio in town. It will be hard work to start with because I will still be teaching at the college, but just think, my own business. Stephen has said he will help, although what with I am not too sure. Maybe accountancy would be a good choice after all.' (I had switched off again with relief knowing she wasn't going away.)

'They are testing a new guillotine in the market square, and I have been chosen as the first one to try it!' 'Oh really?' I said. 'Oh, for heaven's sake, Carrie!' 'I am so sorry, darling. I just thought you were going to say you were moving away too.' 'Wings to fly, Carrie. That's what you said.' 'I know. I know.' 'Well, I am not going far, so can we please start again.'

Charles came in at the end of our conversation. 'What's this about a guillotine?' Phoebe told Charles her good news. 'That's fantastic, Phebes. I am so pleased. Where does the guillotine come in to it?' 'Joke, Charlie, joke.' Phoebe was now getting impatient. 'You explain, Carrie. I have to go and find Stephen.'

We sat in Heathrow airport, a sorry motley crew. Theo apprehensive but excited. Milly jittery as she suddenly realised she didn't know if she would enjoy flying. 'I will just hold on tightly to Tiger's Eyes,' she announced with more confidence than she felt. Phoebe thought how brave of them both to go somewhere alien and not at all too sure what Theo would be doing even if he had explained over and over again. Jack was just glad to get his bedroom to himself again.

I knew if I asked Theo once again if he had their tickets and passports, I would get one of his 'Oh for goodness sake' looks, so I just sat there twiddling my thumbs and dreading their flight call. Charles was sat reading a paper trying to appear nonplussed about the whole thing. He was more optimistic than me. 'It's only for a year, Carrie, but I knew once this company got their hands on my brilliant, son, they wouldn't let him go.' Charles read my thoughts and said, 'You just cannot go off to work in the States willy-nilly, Carrie. There are procedures.' 'Well, I am sure there are loopholes too,' I said rather more bitterly than I intended. 'It is his chance, Carrie.' 'I know, I just wish, it wasn't so far away.' 'Well, we will have to save up and visit when we can.' 'Fat chance of that on our salaries.' Charles looked hurt. 'Oh sorry,' I re-iterated. 'I didn't mean that. I know you work hard. I just feel very jumpy.'

'Will passengers departing on Flight 4059 to New York please go to gate 37?' 'That's us, Tiger's Eyes,' Milly announced and jumped up in anticipation. Theo hugged me in a kind of rigid embrace, shook Charles's hand, hugged his sister, and slapped Jack on the back. 'You all look after yourselves, and we will be in touch soon.' We watched as their rears disappeared through the departure doors with one more quick turn and a wave from them both. Us that remained looked at each other as if our worlds had come to an end.

'Right, home it is then,' Charles was the first to speak. Phoebe was crying. Jack was trying not to. Charles just looked vacant, and I sobbed.

'Come on, Pat,' said when we got home. 'Tea up, and just remember the time will go very quickly.' I didn't tell her what I thought earlier.
A knock at the door heralded the arrival of Stephen. 'I'm off back to work,' Charles said. 'I had better not take advantage of the fact I had leave to go to the airport. Hug please, Carrie Connaught.' 'Kiss please, Charles Jones.' 'Oh, you two,' Phoebe said through the remainder of her tears.

'Stephen and I are going to work out a business plan. Can we use the table, Carrie?' 'Of course. I will continue Jack's lessons in the lounge. I am back in the museum tomorrow, so we need to get through quite a lot today.' I directed at Jack whose face fell down to his boots. Besides which it will take our minds off how quiet the house felt without Milly and her colourful clothes. Theo ever the studious one had been very quiet over the last week, frustrating the hell out of Milly, but I knew she loved him very much and their relationship would work well as long as Theo upped his input into it. I then had an image of Milly skating around an American diner on roller skates which made me smile through my dried up tears.

Jack thought he knew as much as he needed to know already. 'Well, we will see about that young man.' 'I am sure we will, Carrie.' 'You always have to have the last word, Jack.' 'Well, since you have the first half dozen, I have to come in last!' Conversation stopper that one!

Jack had grown into what you could call a handsome lad in a rugged kind of way. He liked his stubble which had just about started to grow. At sixteen, he was still deciding what to do with his life. 'I think I might go to college and take my A levels. I am never going to be a university material and besides which it isn't for me anyway.' He already had his paper round on a Saturday, which precluded an early start to the shack if we decided to go, but that was okay. I was just pleased he had some cash for himself. I suggested he may have grown out of coming with us. 'I don't think so, Carrie. What would Albert do without me?' That thought hadn't crossed my mind. What would he do? Then I thought he had survived before we all descended on him, but he was much younger then, so maybe he really relied on us being there now and again.

I also panicked at the thought of just Charles and me going on our own like Derby and Joan. Jack spoke as I was thinking, 'Don't worry, you will not be on your own for some time to come.'

'Hello, there,' Sheila acknowledged as I walked in to the museum. 'Good news, we have the go-ahead for the tea room! Did they get off okay?' It all came tumbling out at once and between you and me the tea room was the last thing on my mind. 'Hello,' I answered. 'Yes, they did. Thank you. I am still suffering withdrawal symptoms.' 'Well, it is only a day.' Sheila laughed. 'Hello, Mr I Can Do . . . Miller.'

'Morgan actually. Miller is my Christian name.' I felt sorry that for all the time I have worked here, I always thought he was Mr

Miller and realised in that old-age tradition of seafarers, the museum governors had always referred to him as Mr Miller. 'Well, that's confusing,' I thought, two names which could easily be surnames. I comforted myself in the knowledge we didn't cross paths that often and he only came in when we needed a carpenter/handyman. 'Very good he was too,' I might add. We have a galleon and a three mast sailing vessel now proudly displayed with the history of both written up by me. I had to do it several times. Each of the records I looked at had a different story, so I just combined the bits I read and came up with something plausible.

About the tea room, Mary danced up and down all excited. 'It is good news,' I tried to sound pleased. 'And we need to start working on how it will be run.' 'Well, we have funds from the treasurer, so I think nice cups and saucers, teapots and homemade cakes.' I had visions of teaching Jack the history of Richard the Third (which is where we currently are, 'my horse, my horse, my kingdom for a horse,') from the bottom of a mixing bowl.

'I am going to scour the charity shops,' I piped up. 'We don't need matching sets, just some really pretty cups and saucers and some tea plates.' 'Money saving to the end.' Mary laughed. 'Well, you cannot buy really nice ones these days without spending a fortune. It's all mugs which I hate.' 'Me too,' Sheila and Mary chorused. They knew in spite of her appearance which wasn't altogether untidy, just a bit unusual, Carrie had class; however she got the tea room up and running. It would be very special.

'Well, what do you think, Carrie?' Phoebe was proudly displaying hers and Stephen's handiwork. I looked at the projections for years one, two, and three, the figures balanced well, and if it worked out for her, this would be a lucrative business. I know she would put her heart and soul into it. Not too sure about Stephen. 'You haven't allowed too much for advertising, Phoebe.' 'I know, but I can get a deal on the flyers. I just need lots of legs to help me deliver them.' Jack had a 'don't look at me look on his face' hunched on the sofa reading the history of Boadicea which seems to fascinate him. 'I like strong women,' he said.

'Oh really?' Phoebe said. 'In that case, you can offer to help me.' 'Oh, Phebes.' He yawned. 'Do I have to?' 'Oh yes, you do.'

I welcomed this banter to take away the pain of losing Theo and Milly to New York. They must be there by now. I had been hoping for a phone call. Having analysed the situation, they were probably jet-lagged and excited about their new life. I didn't have a number for them, and to be honest, I was not too sure of the time difference. 'We will just have to be patient,' Charles informed me.

I was reluctant to leave the house to go to the shack at the weekend, but Jack said, 'Life has to go on, Carrie. We cannot put ourselves on hold.' 'I know. I just want to know they are safe.' 'Well, if they ring and we are not in, they will try again. They have Pat's number too.'

We collected Freddie whose parents had now mellowed a lot. His father still looked very tired, but he assured us he was okay.

'How is school going, Freddie?' I asked as we sat drinking tea on the wooden steps. 'Not too bad. I really do not know what to do when I leave. My parents want me to stay on, but I just feel I have had enough.' 'Well, you can always come to see me to discuss some options if you would like to. Just ask your parents what they think. We can look at your strong subjects and take it from there.'

'How things have changed,' Carrie thought quietly to herself.

Jack and Freddie went off to kite flying. Charles and I just sat looking at the vast grey ocean and the small boats bobbing up and down on the tide, the late autumnal sun on our faces. No sign of Albert. Jack had checked his hut. 'He is probably out amongst those boats somewhere,' I said. The sea was relatively calm given the stiff breeze. Well his hut's locked, so he probably isn't here today. I wanted to ask him what teacups if any he had on his market stall. I would like to put the money in his pocket as a thank you for everything he does for us, providing supper and looking after our shack and our family.

'Did um get off okay?' a voice boomed in my left ear. Albert appeared from the rear this time. 'Don't do that, Albert. You frightened the life out of me.' 'Sorry, just come down to check. Didn't know u'um would be 'ere.' Jack and Freddie's radar went off. Albert alert shouted Jack over the noise of the breaking waves. They saw him in the distance and ran back to say hello.

After nearly knocking each other over, Albert said, 'Come on, ur two varmints, I will show you how to cast a line.' Jack and Freddie went off with Albert to his hut for hours of beach fishing.

Left on our own again, Charles and I made use of this rare time to ourselves. We discussed Theo and his new job, which neither of us fully understood, Phoebe's business plan, and Jack's future. We also talked about the future of the shack. Were we going to come here on our own, probably for a while, as we decided, whether to close it up or not? Really it had served its purpose for us and our growing family. They had grown up in this isolated, barren wasteland with dear Albert with us all the way. 'I'm getting maudlin,' I said to Charles. 'Me too,' he said. 'Come on, let's go and see if they have caught anything.' When we eventually found them some way along the water's edge, Albert's first words were, 'U'um got a frying pan, Missus? It be too late to fire up that old tin can o' 'urs.' We all wandered back to the shack.
'Well done, boys. Let's get cooking.' Albert had done the necessary to their caught fish.

We sat watching the sun set over the horizon and the dusk slowly creeping in. Jack and Freddie were deciding whether to go for more kite flying. 'It be a bit dark, lads,' Albert said. 'Yes and a bit chilly,' I muted.

'Albert, do you have any nice cups and saucers on your market stall?' 'Wha' u'um wanna know afor?' I smiled at his suspicious tone. 'Because we are opening a tea room in the museum where I work and we are looking for some china.' 'China what?' 'Cups, saucers, and tea plates.' 'Might 'av.' 'Well, if you might have, Albert, can we come and see you one day? I would like to buy some if possible.' 'Well, I be there moro if u'um be interested.' 'Tomorrow it is then.' Charles sighed. 'We are not equipped to stay here tonight. No blankets, hot water bottles, and food, so we will come back and meet you in the market square.' 'Okay, that be fine wi me.' Jack smiled to himself. He sometimes thought Albert seemed like a dafter and more stubborn version of Theo.

Albert was quick witted and savvy but could be very awkward sometimes.

We took Freddie home, which was a waste of time, because the minute he went in the door, he asked his mother if he could stay the night with us and come to the market. She said yes. He came running out before our antiquated rust heap had departed, shouting he was coming with us. Five minutes later, pyjamas and toothbrush in hand, he came out again, sat in the back of our car, and said, 'Right, home, James.' 'It's Charlie.' 'Okay, home, Charlie.' 'Cheeky beggar,' Charles said under his breath.

Pat came running in. Well, not quite running, just flustered. 'Theo phoned, Carrie and Charlie. He is very sorry he missed you and will try again. They have lovely accommodation, a flat in a large complex not far from the laboratories where he is working. He said he has met his boss who seems quite pleasant, but time will tell. He starts work on Monday, but if he doesn't have time to phone, he will write and tell you all about everything. Milly is starting a job hunt too. I have his number for you and they are four hours behind us.' 'Phew, thanks, Pat. Sit down. I will make us tea.' (I was so relieved to hear Theo and Milly had reached safely and would make a conscious effort to contact my son one way or the other.) We need to get warm. I related the story of the museum tea room and the visit tomorrow to Albert's market stall. 'Good luck with that one.' Pat giggled. 'Thanks, my friend, that was!' 'Oh, you don't mean that, Carrie.' 'No, I don't.'

Everything changes and everything stays the same. These words crossed my mind. I was not good with change of any sort, the money side or circumstances. I was a Cancerian (not that I believe in that rubbish), but I never resist a sneaky peak at the astrologer's column in the paper when I get the chance.

We were up bright and early the following morning to make our way to the market square and Albert's stall. He was sat there puffing away on his pipe as usual, grunting to himself about something we couldn't quite hear.

'Well, wha' u'um want from this lot then?' 'Wow, Albert, these are gorgeous,' I gushed and meant it. A cardboard box holding the most exquisite china I had ever seen, apart from mine that is. 'Where did you find this?' I asked. 'Ne'er u'um mind,' he said in his usual way. 'I ne'er says where I gets me stuff from, so don't u'um ask.' 'Righto,' Charles said. 'Do you want it, Carrie?' 'Was Sidney Poitier the most wonderful actor? What on earth had he got to do with it? I didn't know you had a thing for him.' 'Oh . . . do you know what? I cannot explain myself all the time!'

'How much Albert?' 'You u'um avin the lot then?' 'Yes please,' I said. 'They not be machin cups and stuff.' 'I know that Albert. That's why I love it.' "Ow does a fiver the lot sound to e then?' I pressed a ten-pound note into his fisherman's blistered and worn hands. 'I get e change,' he said, fumbling in his pocket. 'I don't want any change, Albert.' "Y, thankee, missus. I be very grateful. U'um want them there teapots too?' 'Yes please, Albert. Thank you.' 'One's got a lid what don't match but it fit okay.'

'Not as grateful as I am, Albert. Now, I am looking for cutlery, knives, teaspoons that kind of thing.' 'I knows what cutlery is, missus? 'im over there sells it.'

We left the market loaded with everything I needed for the tea room. I went to say goodbye to Albert who sat on his stool by his stall looking tired and a bit dejected. 'What's the matter, Albert?' 'Well, you taken most o' me stuff I got nuffin left to sell.' 'Isn't that what you want to do, Albert, sell it?' 'Spose it is. What appens now I ain't got much to do. I didn't know whether to laugh or cry.' This old sea dog I loved with my life had more money in his pocket than he would have got selling to anyone else, yet he was worried he hadn't anything left. I had also bought three foldaway card tables from him we could use. These were not the flimsy kind and had been very expensive in their days.

'Early doors for you then, Albert. You can go home and have a nice cup of tea.' 'No, I can't. The missus won't want me under her feet all day.'

Charles nudged me. 'Let's load the car,' he said, 'and go and find a cafe.' 'Okay,' I said relieved. 'Come on, Albert. We can go for a cup of tea.' 'Nows u'um talkin. Keep an eye on wots left 'ere, Derek,' he shouted to the cutlery man. 'Righto, Albert.' To be honest, what he had left really wasn't worth keeping half an eye on, a few old rickety chairs and a box of old rusty tools.

'Keep a look out for a librarian with a pudding basin haircut,' I whispered to Charles. 'We still have their books.' 'I know but they won't be worth giving back now and who knows what the fine would be.' We hadn't meant to be book thieves, but somehow just didn't get around to taking them back.

Thank goodness, we didn't see anyone remotely resembling Mrs Library lady! We took Albert to the nearest cafe, settled him in the corner by the window, and ordered tea for him and coffee for us. We decided on three pieces of Victoria sponge and settled down to listen to some more of Albert's tales before heading home.

CHAPTER THIRTEEN
Carrie

'Good afternoon, Mansford Pharmaceuticals, Amanda speaking.' 'Oh, is it?' I said. 'Sorry, it's morning here.' I was all of a fluster and couldn't quite get my words out. 'Can I speak to Theo Jones, please.' 'Who may I ask is calling?' the happy-clappy voice echoed down the line. 'Tell him it's Carrie, please.' 'Carrie, who?' I was aware this call was costing us an arm and a leg. 'It is Carrie Connaught, his mother,' I said through clenched teeth. Her sing-songy voice and American accent were grating on bits I didn't know I had.

'Theo Jones, here,' my son already displayed a slight American drawl. 'Hi, Theo.' 'Hi, Carrie, sorry I didn't realise it was you. The receptionist couldn't hear you properly.' 'How are you, Theo, and how is the job going.' 'Fine and fine, Carrie. How is everyone?' 'We are doing okay. Great to speak to you at last. We had tried several times but seemed to miss each other.' I handed the phone to Charles. 'Hi, son, you doing okay?' 'Hi, Charlie, yes. Thank you. And you?' 'Well, in between work, painting your mother's new tea room in the museum, and buying china from Albert's stall, which was a bit like pulling teeth, I am fine. Phoebe is busy with her Theatre company, and Jack is at Freddie's.' 'Sorry, we haven't caught up with each other. I am busy at the moment writing a research paper,' Theo said, which sounded all too complicated for Charles's ears. 'Well done, son,' he said. 'Let us know how it goes,' knowing full well he wouldn't understand any of it.

'Hi, it's Carrie again.' Theo repeated what he had said to Charles. 'I will send you a copy once it's finished, Carrie.' 'Thank you very much. I would love that. Write soon and take care. Is Milly still on roller blades?' 'Yep,' Theo answered, 'and loving it.' 'Give her our love.

We miss you both so much.' I was hoping for a 'miss you too,' but didn't get it. 'Bye for now. Speak soon.'

Close to the edge of tears, I replaced the receiver with a clunk.

It doesn't get any easier this long-distance relationship with our son. 'Wings to fly,' I muttered to myself.

'Come on, Carrie, the shack calls,' Charles said, trying to cheer me up. We wrote a quick note for Phoebe and Jack. I made sandwiches and packed a flask this time and took a tin of soup out of the cupboard. Freddie and Jack had eaten the homemade chicken, the one I made yesterday.

We sat side by side in the warm spring sunshine watching the gulls play havoc with the small fishing vessels on the horizon. Why are they so greedy? Seagulls must be the most overfed species on the planet. We had watched them steal food from people's hands on several occasions. They could also be quite vicious.

'Do you ever regret attaching yourself to me, Caroline Connaught?' 'What an odd question, Charles? Where did that come from?' 'Well, I haven't had a lot to offer . . .' 'Stop it right there. You have given me three beautiful children and a fairly comfortable life. I had a choice, and I made the right one. How about you Charles Jones?' Charles scratched his chin and looked at me with a sparkle in his blue eyes. 'You will do till something better comes along.' If it hadn't been so far to the water's edge, I would have filled a bucket and chucked it over him.

A squelch of wellingtons in wet silt made us both jump. 'U'um look like o' pair o' abandoned rag bags' 'Oh really, well you look like a sack of something the tide washed up.' 'No change thur then. Any tea goin', missus?' I pulled out a chair for Albert. 'Sit there and be quiet,' I said in my best school ma'am voice. 'W'ere be them young varmints got to then.' 'Not so young anymore, Albert. Jack and Freddie are studying this afternoon. I hope I will have some work to mark when I get back. Phoebe is working hard on her new business venture.'

''Ows that there tea room comin' along.' 'Great, thanks. The china is beautiful. I have to say there was a fair amount of dead flies and spiders in the cups. We had to thoroughly wash everything but worth it in the end. The governors of the museum are extremely pleased, although I am sure they will find something to moan about given time!'

I explained to Albert we had spoken to Theo, but it went over his head. Anything outside huts, fishing, and mending nets was out of his comfort zone. Conversation was thin on the ground about anything else. Oh and his market stall! It wasn't that he didn't care about Theo. It was more he didn't understand why anyone would want to travel to a foreign country as he put it.

'U'um got any spare cake? The missus don't make any since er bin poorly.' I gave Albert some cake and said, 'We really ought to be getting back. I still have some ironing to do and to see what Jack and Freddie had been up to. Back to the grind tomorrow for Charles and me.'

I put our dishes and flask back in a carrier bag to take home to wash.

Albert said he was going to his hut to tidy up a bit and may take his boat out for an hour or so if it stays calm. 'I be a fair weather fisherman these days. I don't 'ave the stomach for anythin' rough anymore.' 'Okay, Albert. Take care. See you soon.'

We walked hand in hand back to what is loosely called our car. And Charles drove us home. I felt much better for being out and have put things in to perspective as far as Theo was concerned. We were all still on the same planet and could communicate so that was all that matters.

'Hi, Carrie. Hi, Charlie.' I read Theo's airmail letter a million times. Well, not quite, a bit of an exaggeration, but lots of times, mainly through tears. 'I have been asked to stay on,' he wrote. 'Lots of official paperwork to sort out, but it's a chance I cannot pass up. Milly wants to stay too, so although I know you probably won't be very happy, I hope you will be pleased for us.' 'Wings to fly,' I said to myself again. It was the mantra that helps me through not having our son here.

I wished I had Charles's philosophical outlook. He was as proud as a peacock. Me too if I wanted to be honest, and I supposed a little bit of me always thought this would happen. Why would they want to let go of my great son?

'You only have yourself to blame, Caroline Connaught?' Charles said, reading my thoughts as he hugged me tightly. 'You put him on the road to stardom. You erected the board from which he dived into the sea of life.'

Maybe one day we would be able to go and see him. I knew we probably wouldn't, but that thought helped ease my aching heart. Besides which when did my 'Tony Curtis lookalike' get to be so profound!

Phoebe came in hotly followed by Stephen. She took one look at my face and was immediately worried. 'It's okay,' I said and relayed Theo's news. 'Well done him,' she said with the exuberance of youth. She obviously hadn't realised the enormity of not seeing her brother.

'Well, I have good news,' she said. It all came tumbling out, her big blue eyes seeking approval first from Charles and then me. 'Stephen and I are going to rent another studio. We have done very well as you know and we need to expand. This one is in London. Well, the outskirts really, a rundown place which will need a lot of work, and we are looking to finance it through the monies from the workshop here plus a loan. We also want to employ someone to run this one for us whilst we get the London one up and running.' 'Phoebe, I am so very pleased for you. Well done. Stephen, we always thought you would make a better accountant than a dancer.' 'Really?' he said, shock horror written all over his face. 'Whatever gave you that idea!'

To recap. The Connaught/Jones family. Theo Jones, research analyst; Phoebe Jones, business woman extraordinaire; Jack Jones, well not too sure on that one yet. Charles Jones still supervising the pickle and chutney conveyor belt; Caroline Connaught, museum curator come tutor, tea lady, and cake maker. 'Oh and I forgot, we have the shack which will probably be our retirement home if things don't change!'

Sheila looked a bit nonplussed when I announced Theo's intentions at work. Mary wasn't too sure what to say. 'Did I sound like bragging? I hope not. Maybe it all came out the wrong way.'

'Sorry, Carrie,' Sheila said. 'It's a mixed blessing for you. I am sure. I know how much you miss Theo. Well done him,' Mary said. I could tell her heart wasn't in it.

'Okay, girls, what is going on?' 'Nothing, Carrie.' 'Come on,' I said, 'spill!' 'It's Miller. He is leaving us.' 'Oh is that all.' I didn't mean to sound so insensitive. 'No, that is not all,' Sheila said sharply. 'He is ill, Carrie, very ill.' 'This is all very sudden,' I said to cover up my surprise. 'I am so sorry to hear that. Is there anything we can do to help him?' 'His wife and family are looking after him very well. I think they are managing okay.'

I supposed in hindsight, Sheila and Mary worked more closely with Miller than I did. I was upset obviously and annoyed at myself for being so dismissive. I felt as if the stability in my life was like a crumbling floor waiting to swallow me up. 'Don't be so selfish, Carrie,' I admonished myself. 'Miller is ill. The last thing you should be doing is thinking of yourself. But I do.'

I was unsure whether the governors would replace him given funding from the local council was practically non-existent.

We opened the tea room, sliced, and arranged the cakes we had made for that day. Mine an apple upside down, Mary had made a fruit one, and Sheila a Victoria sponge. It hadn't risen much, but it looked edible. 'I told you, I am not a baker,' Sheila said, looking at the telltale expression on my face. 'I am sure it will taste good,' I said kindly.

'I will run things today if you like,' Sheila said. 'I need to be busy. That's fine.' I have loads of paperwork and some secret marking for Jack's work too. The governors would not be too happy if they knew I had brought my children's school work with me to mark over the years. It was the only way I could keep up with everything. Besides which I needed to really study Theo's work at the time. Jack and Phoebe were easier because they did as I asked, so I knew more or less what to expect from their work.

Judging by the clatter of teacups and plates, the tea room is a success. Some people seemed to ignore the exhibits and just headed straight through to the cafe. That is only to be expected, I supposed. Tea and cakes were a good magnet, and if they brought us more visitors, that could only be a good thing. More visitors mean more funding apparently. The level of people coming through the door had increased considerably in the last few years, but I hadn't seen much extra money. I didn't want to rock the boat and ask for more. The trustees were a crusty old bunch. During our quarterly meetings, I normally had to wake most of them up to get a conversation flowing.

I did get the odd well done for the amount of hard work my team and I had put in but that was as far as it went. I was grateful that our efforts were recognised in some way.

CHAPTER FOURTEEN
Carrie

If Jack had still been five years old, I would have understood his next comment. I had asked what he wanted to do career-wise. 'I am going to be a fisherman like Albert,' he retorted. 'Oh really, and how do you propose to do that?' 'I don't know. I just fancy it!' 'Right, well, going out to sea in all weathers, come rain or shine, calm or a hurricane, is not something you can just fancy doing.'

'Keep your hair on, Carrie, I am joking. I have an interview with Drayton Electronics this afternoon. They are looking for an apprentice.'

Well, that shut me up for a while. I eventually found my tongue again. 'You kept that quiet, lad,' I said when I got my breath back. 'Well, I wanted to surprise you.' 'You have certainly done that. What time do you have to be there?' I asked. 'I have been summoned at 2.30 p.m.' 'I would go earlier if I was you, Jack. It is a huge building, and it would be good to familiarise yourself with the layout before you meet the big boss.' 'Good idea, Carrie. Thank you for that. Great advice as usual. It isn't all fresh air up there then,' Jack said, touching my head. 'Away with you and again good luck!'

'Come in, lad.' Mr Drayton was almost dwarfed by his desk. 'Please take a seat.' ('Where to?' Jack thought to himself, and the inward smile calmed his nerves.)

'Right, tell me about yourself.' Jack wasn't too sure where to start, so he said, 'My name is Jack Jones. Eighteen years old, living at Tennyson Crescent, and have a Saturday paper round.' 'And?' Mr Drayton said, shuffling papers across his desk. 'Well, I am looking for work as soon as possible and would hope you would consider me for your scheme.' 'Education?' Mr Drayton said quite sharply. 'Phew,' Jack said to himself, 'this is difficult.' 'I am home schooled by my mother

Carrie who has a degree in Mathematics and Art. I have learnt a great deal. Indeed, my brother went to Oxford University and is currently working in the States on a research project.' 'Was he home schooled too?' 'Yes and my sister, who has her own dance and theatre company.'

'Well done, Mrs Jones, then. She has done a very good job.' 'Actually, it's Carrie, Carrie Connaught. She is the curator of the local maritime museum.' 'Oh really, well any way, well done her.'

'I want enthusiasm and dedication and in return, we will put you on the road to success. You start on the shop floor and work your way through all the different trades available.' 'I am interested in design,' Jack replied, 'but I am very willing to learn.' 'That's what I like to hear, Mr Jones. Come to my office next Monday at 8.30 a.m. sharp, and we will get you started. This is an apprenticeship. The pay will reflect that. Work hard, lad, and you will be well rewarded eventually.'

'Thank you very much, Mr Drayton. I will not let you down.' Jack had never been called Mr Jones before and it seemed weird. 'But I expect I will get used to it,' he thought to himself.

'You will be pleased to know, Carrie. Your youngest and favourite offspring is now employed.' 'That is fantastic news, Jack. Well done, you. I am so proud. Just wait till we tell Charles when he gets home.'

'I am off to tell Pat,' Jack shouted as he went out the door. He came back laughing saying he thought she was going to eat him alive; she was so pleased.

Flipping heck was Charlie's response. 'What great news! Well done, son. Thank you.' 'It just seems odd being called, Mr Jones.'

'Just thank your lucky stars if that is all you are called! I was "do you ever get it right?" when I first started at the pickle factory. And a few choice names since. Employment law is changing, son. It is a much better time to start a new job now than when I did.'

ALBERT HAD DIED, SORRY. These words were written on a scrap of paper stuck to the door of his hut.

We had gone to the shack with Phoebe and Jack to say hello to Albert whom we hadn't seen for a while. Jack had wandered over to see if he was around to tell him about his apprenticeship and came back as white as a sheet. 'He has gone, Carrie.' 'Gone, where, Jack?' He took us all over to show us the note. 'Oh dear!' We all just stood there wondering what to do or say next. We didn't know where he lived or very much about him. He had been so much part of our family, but we knew so little about his life. In hindsight, that was the way he seemed to want things to be. 'I wonder who wrote this,' I said pointing to the note. It was very short and to the point, possibly Mrs Albert or another fisherman.

'We could see if there are any other fishermen around who might know.' Even as I said it, I knew there wouldn't be, and there never usually was.

We locked the shack and walked in to the town to see if we could glean any information. Nobody seemed to know anything. We asked in the cafe we had taken Albert to the day we bought his china. They were none the wiser.

We bought a bunch of flowers and a card and took them back to our shack. We put our names and telephone number on the card asking if whoever found them could contact us and attached the card to the flowers and placed them by the door of Albert's hut.

We were all shell-shocked and wanting to go home. We told Pat our news and sat down to write to Theo and Milly. Pat was very upset even though she didn't know Albert very well. 'He was such a character,' she said through tears of sadness.

We didn't hear a thing from anyone, so we decided to have our own little service for Albert. Stephen came too, although he didn't know him. He was there for Phoebe really. The flowers and card we had left before were still there outside Albert's hut. We collected them up to throw away. The flowers had long since died, and obviously, no one had seen them, or if they had, had decided to ignore our note. At home, we had collected things from our garden and made a wreath from oak leaves and laurel intertwined them with a few daisies and some ribbon.

'God bless, Albert,' we said in unison as we tossed the wreath into the outgoing tide. We stood and watched it bobbing up and down on the crest of the wave and turned away each in our own little world. 'I will put the kettle on,' Jack said. 'We can have some tea before we head home.' 'Good idea, son. Thank you.' Charles hugged me. I hugged Jack and Phoebe, and Stephen hugged each other.

Somehow the chill wind which blew across this stark landscape felt colder than ever. It was fun before wrapping up against the blustery gales, laughing, running, playing games, and generally enjoying the freedom here. Now, I felt desolate. I sensed we all did. It would never be the same again. Perhaps the time had come to say goodbye to our seaside home.

'What sad news!' Theo wrote. 'I suppose it was bound to happen sometime but not quite as suddenly as this. My love and thoughts are with you all.' He wrote about lots of other news, mainly work related, and a well done to Jack, wishing him all the best in his new job. 'Take care, Love Theo and Milly xx.'

In time, we came to accept Albert's passing and realised he wouldn't want us to give up our shack. With all our children grown up and gainfully employed, Charles and I would probably go alone most of the time. Where had all the years gone?

A year later, I still hadn't had word from Theo about his research paper. 'These things take time, Carrie,' he wrote when I asked about it. I sensed the frustration in his letters. We hadn't been able to reach him by phone, so we relied on the written word to communicate.

A knock at the front door frightened me out of my wits. It broke into my thoughts as I was getting ready for bed. Charles and Jack had already gone upstairs. Jack was shattered most of the time. He was pushed quite hard with his job, but he enjoyed it very much. Phoebe and Stephen were renting near their new studio, but we saw a lot of them as they oversaw their local one as well.

'Hey, it's me.' Milly jumped in through the front door hardly giving me time to open it properly, hotly followed by her backpack. 'Good heavens! What are you doing here? Is everything okay?' 'Great,' she said, hugging the breath out of me. 'I have been to see Mummy and Daddy, and guess what, I am meeting up with Theo. He is on his way as we speak.' 'What!' I exclaimed. 'It was supposed to be a surprise, but I have blown it now arriving first.' Charles and Jack came down the stairs yawning wondering what the commotion was. 'Look, who is here,' I shouted, feeling absolutely elated. 'And Theo is on his way too. He should be here tomorrow. That was why his letters seemed a little distant. He didn't want to give the game away.'

'Why didn't you come over together?' 'Well, I needed to see Mummy. She hasn't been too well, but I wanted to be here too, so I thought it best to come a few days earlier. I cannot believe Albert has gone,' Milly said and seemed even more overwhelmed than we were.

'I will make some tea. Are you hungry, Milly?' 'Not really, thank you. I had supper at Mummy and Daddy's. A drink would be good though.'

We sat around for a while drinking tea and exchanging stories. 'I really miss Tiger's Eyes. I cannot wait to see him again.' Milly had a dreamy look in her eyes, probably partly tiredness as well.

'You can have Phoebe's room. The bed is made up. She visits us a lot but doesn't stay so much any more.'

'I don't expect I will sleep much. I am too excited.' 'You and me both,' I thought. Charles and Jack couldn't believe Theo was on his way. It was just the lift this family of mine needed right now.

CHAPTER FIFTEEN
Carrie and Jack

Bright and early the next morning, the house shone like a new pin. Carrie had been up for hours dusting and polishing waiting for her son to arrive.

His plane was due in at 7 a.m. but by the time he came through customs and picked up his hire car, which would take a while as he would be driving on a licence obtained in the States, this would need to be checked out, so we reckoned he would be with us around 11 a.m. depending on the traffic.

Milly was hanging over the garden gate at 10.30. She hadn't changed one bit. Her hair still a mass of unkempt curls and her clothes as colourful as ever. She still worked in the all-American diner which she loved, mainly the roller blades, which she had become expert on apparently. 'Well, I suppose you would have to be pretty good balancing trays of food as well.'

A car pulled up, and Theo got out and swept Milly off her feet. 'Where are my family?' he shouted, carrying her up to the front door.

I opened the door and said, 'Welcome home, son,' with a trembling voice. I was trying really hard not to cry. I knew that would probably annoy him. 'Hi, Carrie.' Charles came to the door and shook his son's hand. 'Welcome home, Theo.' 'Good to see you, Charlie. Where is that annoying brother of mine then?' he asked, looking over our shoulders. 'Here,' Jack said, 'I thought I would leave you all to greet each other. Then I might get a word in edgeways. I have missed you big brother, but at least I have my room to myself.' 'Great,' Theo said. 'Good to see you too, brother. Where is my flighty sister?' 'She

105

will be round later, Theo,' Charlie said, feeling a growing excitement at having all of his family together again.

My all-American son had grown in stature and looked well even after the long flight.

'I cannot believe you are here,' I said, not for the first time. 'Well we have a few days, so although I know you will all be at work, we will see a fair amount of each other.' 'Too true,' I said. 'I will pass on some work to Mary and make sure I only do my part-time hours.'

'So sad about Albert,' Theo said as he settled in what used to be his favourite armchair by the window. 'I just wish we could find out more, but we have drawn a blank so far.' 'Best not delve in to things too much, Carrie. I think Albert would like us to respect his privacy.' The voice of reason, Theo was right as usual. 'We had our own private little send off for him,' I told Theo, 'and a home-made wreath.' 'Well, that is all you can do, and I am sure he would be very happy with that.'

'Would it be insensitive if I asked to go to the shack?' Milly asked almost in a whisper. I thought for a moment and said, 'No, of course not. Albert would not want us to put our lives on hold. We will go this weekend. Maybe Sunday would be best. Charles sometimes works Saturday mornings.' 'Great,' said Milly, a smile spreading across her face.

We congregated outside our wooden haven: Theo, Phoebe, Jack, Milly, Stephen, Charles, and me.
An air of sadness hung over us like a cloud. Stephen seemed mesmerised by the whole thing. Milly was clinging to Theo's arm. I made us hot chocolate, and we sat outside taking in the cool air and thinking of that old sea dog we had all come to love, except Stephen, of course, who hadn't met him.
'Tell me about your job, Jack.' Theo broke the silence with his question. 'Well, it is going well, moving up the ladder so to speak. I don't sweep floors or make the tea any more. I am now in the design department which was my goal.' The conversation then got very

technical, but it sounded to me as if Jack was designing a new circuit board which would be of universal use for many electrical things. Some of which I had never heard of. The prototype was being built in the factory as a test piece. Mr Drayton still harrumphed behind his enormous desk but said to Jack one day last week, 'You have done us proud, lad.' I would echo that.

I looked around at my family and knew the choices Charles and I had made were the right ones. It was very hard to come to terms with the changes going on around us, losing Albert, our children all grown up and successful, wishing not for the first time Theo had brought his success closer to home.

They were happy and healthy which was really all we wanted for them. Everything else was a bonus.

'God bless you, Albert,' we said as we raised our cups in a joint salute.

Charles was the first to move. He wandered over to what was left of Albert's hut. Nothing was there. The door was open, but the inside was bare. I rarely saw Charles cry, but the enormity of the empty hut brought everything home to him. 'I feel so sad,' he muttered when he walked back.

'Come on,' Milly broke the moment. 'Let's have a wander and see what we can find. The first one to see a crab gets to wash the cups.' 'Well, no one is going to volunteer for that.' I laughed. She had succeeded in bringing some sunshine in to our day.

We ran and skipped our way along the water's edge. Charles was holding my hand in a rare display of public togetherness. Apart from the time at Theo's graduation for Lord and Lady Marriot's benefit.

All too soon our time with Theo and Milly was up. They had to get back to their lives and jobs.

'Bye, everyone,' Theo and Milly shouted as their car moved out of our short driveway. 'Bye, bye,' we called back. 'Have a good flight and let us know when you are back safely.' 'Will do. Love you all.' 'We love you too.'

Over the next couple of years, we lost Pat. Her family suddenly appeared to clear out and sell her home. In their defence, they did come to see us and asked if there was anything we would like for a keepsake? I chose a brooch which I had always admired. I also took back my teacup and saucer with the ivy painted around the rim. Really surprised it was still in one piece, well, two actually, I did say cup and saucer! After my son went to work in the States and we lost Albert, a kind of immunity built up and the loss of Pat just produced a numbness I felt for sometime dreading coming back to reality.

I began to value my family even more: Charlie, Theo, Phoebe, and Jack. Our lives continued in much the same way as before. I still worked in the museum. Charlie still packed pickles and chutney. Our children had really outshone us, and we carried a lot of pride in them and knew they were doing the very things they had chosen to do.

We had new neighbours, a young couple who seemed extremely strange at first. They eyed us up and down on our first meeting. 'Mark and Catrina, pleased to meet you.' 'Carrie and Charles,' I answered. I did smile to myself as Catrina's eyes settled on Charles rather longer than was necessary. Charles was still handsome. Hair more grey but still my 'Tony Curtis lookalike'.

'We have a son at home,' I ventured. 'Hopefully you will meet him soon.' At the same time, I wondered when Jack would leave and have a place of his own. 'I think we have him for some time.' Charles laughed reading my thoughts.

Well, he was right. Jack was at home for a few more years but managed to secure a London apartment overlooking the Thames. His success with Drayton Electronics had gone from strength to strength. He had secured a place on the board after Mr Drayton senior passed away.

'Well, what do you think, Carrie and Charlie?' Jack showed us round his new apartment with pride. 'I love it,' I said with a voice tinged with sadness. My youngest son was leaving us for pastures new. 'It is only just down the road,' Charles said again, reading my thoughts. 'I know,' I answered, realising we had two of our children living within a short distance.

Phoebe was happily settled with Stephen, and their business was doing well. We had regular visits and went to see them often.

The shack? Well, we were finding it difficult. Growing older, we were no longer comfortable in the bunks and really felt the cold. Charles and I did go occasionally more for the peace and quiet than anything else. It was amazing how age changes you. I never ever thought when my children were small that the time would come when we preferred our home comforts. We found our thoughts wandering as we sat on the steps outside our wooden pied-à-terre, mainly our children playing here with not a care in the world and Albert. 'We have been very lucky, Carrie Connaught.' 'Well, luck paid a huge part, but so did hard work.'

Freddie had become a bit of a drifter. He started working in the local shoe shop. That didn't work, so he decided to go off travelling. How he found the money, we don't know, but he was gone for months at a time. He and Jack were still the best of friends, and knowing Jack, he will sort something out for Freddie if he decided to stay in one place long enough. I had expected more from Freddie. I put in a fair few hours with him trying to help him career-wise. I knew some time ago it wasn't going to work and he was going to do his own thing anyway, but I still tried. I sometimes wondered if his parents thought our lifestyle had contributed to his nomadic ways. If they did, they never said.

CHAPTER SIXTEEN
Carrie

'Get yourselves a passport each,' Jack announced on his last visit. 'You are off to see Theo before you are too old and decrepit.' 'How can we do that, Jack, we cannot afford the flights?' 'Well, Phebes and I can, so we are going.' 'Oh my goodness!' Charles went as white as a sheet. 'Neither of us had flown before. You can't do that,' I said, feeling all of a sudden extremely excited and scared in equal measures. 'Oh yes, we can. Remember, Carrie, I always have the last word.'

Sitting at the airport with Charles, Jack, and Phoebe, I mulled over the expression on the trustees' faces at the museum when I told them I was off for three weeks. 'You can't do that.' 'I can, and am,' I retorted. Whether I had a job when I get back was another story. Mary and Sheila, who like me were no spring chickens, were holding the fort so to speak. Charles's boss was more understanding. 'You haven't had a holiday. Well, a proper one in years, Charlie. You go and enjoy yourself.' Phoebe's business was left in Stephen's capable hands. He still had two left feet but Phoebe had already employed a very good teacher, so Stephen was only responsible for the finances.

We had been to the shack, collected a few things, and locked it up not really knowing when we would go back there again. I said to Charles to collect my china and tray, but he had forgotten, and I remember thinking maybe it was his way of saying we would be back to spend some time there.

New York was all Theo and Milly said it would be: colourful, loud, and very busy. I don't know about Charles, but I felt a bit like a fish out of water. 'Don't get me wrong,' Carrie wrote in her journal. 'I love every minute of it and was so proud to be introduced to Theo's boss and told something of his work.' The research paper was still not finished after all this time. 'I am so busy, Carrie, and I like to spend my time off with Milly, we can do things together.'

I wanted to ask Theo if he and Milly were getting married, but I knew my son well enough not to. They were still so right for each other, and at the risk of incurring his wrath even more, I wanted to ask if we would be grandparents any time soon. Neither question passed my lips, and Charles had already said, 'Best not to ask, Carrie. We will know soon enough if there is any news about either.'

We loved spending time with our son, and Charles seemed very knowledgeable about New York having read the book I had bought for us so at least we would have some idea about the places we visited. We didn't dare visit any more libraries after the last encounter.

We had a meal in the diner served by Milly on her blades. We laughed till we cried watching her speed around the expansive room filled with tables and chairs looking like something out of the 1950s. The decor that was not Milly, I hastened to add, although . . .

'Thank you so much everyone for making this possible,' Charles said, his blue eyes clearer and shinier than I had seen them for a long time. 'Yes, amen to that,' I cut in. 'Well, you deserve it, Carrie and Charlie, after all you have done for us.' At the risk of this scene sounding maudlin and a little cheesy, I said, 'Let's go and see the Statue of Liberty.' 'Not me,' Charles said, 'I don't like heights.' 'Well, you can always wait for us unless there is somewhere else you would like to go.'

Milly had finished her shift, so Theo suggested a walk around Central Park which we could see from Theo and Milly's flat.

What a fantastic few days we had! The shops were enormous and very expensive. Come to think of it, everything seemed a lot bigger than at home. We enjoyed window-shopping, which was an art in itself in New York. The displays were wonderful. Some shops had managed to turn their windows into stories. My favourite one was a children's book shop which had all the characters from *The Wind in the Willows* displayed. They looked almost real, except Ratty, of course. I hoped I would never see a rat that size!

How do you sum it all up? I was not really too sure. My family were not conventional, but somehow everything had turned out well. Who would have thought we would be spending time in America? No one could foretell the future, and even if they could, how would it even be possible to predict the Connaught/Jones family turning out this way?

We returned to the UK with a mixture of sadness and elation. We could now picture Theo and Milly's life and were very grateful to our children for the most fantastic time. No Pat to welcome us back. I still hadn't got used to not having her around. How she would have loved to listen to stories about our trip! And she would have laughed over the fact that for once in his life, Charles did not look particularly good (as most of us don't) in his passport photo. As for me, well, the least said about that one the better. It was too late to phone Theo and Milly, so we made a mental note to call in the morning to say we were all home safe and sound and to say thank you again.

I opened the front door thinking I had heard a tentative knock. Laid against the wall was a bouquet with a note saying, 'Welcome home, everyone. Love from Catrina and Mark x.' 'Thank you,' I whispered as I picked up the beautiful flowers.

CHAPTER SEVENTEEN
Jack

There was no choice where Carrie and Charlie were concerned. Both elderly and afflicted by various ailments, it was down to me to move back home to care for them. Actually, I volunteered if you want the truth. (I had unpaid time off from my job, coupled with compassionate leave.) They were not going to be parted or looked after by some stranger who wouldn't or couldn't understand them. I had no ties except my job. I was still able to commute to the office from time to time to check everything was running smoothly. It invariably did. Girls had come and gone but no one special at the moment.

With the help of a nurse and our family doctor, they lived out their lives in a relative pain-free comfort and security, and when they finally said goodbye to each other and passed away with just a couple of months between them (Carrie went first), we were touched by a sadness which was hard to bear.

I phoned Theo who had kept in touch through telephone calls and letters. He couldn't hide the tears I knew were flowing. Phoebe had come home to stay on several occasions to help me and spend time with us. Like her, Theo was going to struggle to come to terms with losing our parents.

It was very strange not to know very much about Charlie's background. 'My life started when I met your mother,' he always said. If Carrie knew anything, she never had mentioned it.

We then found out our parents had never married. That was a shock! How did we not know! It would explain why Carrie always avoided replying when we asked why they had different surnames. Her answer was, 'My name is who I am.' Charlie always just shrugged his shoulders when asked.

After the funerals (they were cremated), Phebes, Theo, and I spent time together before they returned to their lives and jobs. I volunteered to stay behind and clear up what remained of the odds and ends. What little 'family money' we had was shared between us after the funeral expenses. Phebes had Carrie's jewellery. Theo and I shared Charlie's tiepins and cufflinks which he had collected over the years and treasured. I gave Pat's brooch to Theo to take back for Milly. She had been very sensitive about everything, and although she wanted to be here for Theo, she elected to stay behind in New York saying it was a family time, but her thoughts were with us all. I cleared the house of what was left of our possessions, ready to hand back to the council who were kind, giving us time to grieve and sort everything out.

Sadness overwhelmed us all, but somehow the memories good and not so good were enhanced in retrospect. I needed to visit the shack one last time, and then it was time to move on as Carrie and Charlie would want us all to do.

I approached the wooden door with trepidation, a rusty key swinging from my fingers.
This was just one time when I was uncertain and a little scared. Up two rickety steps which surprised me by holding my weight, a sandy-surfaced wooden platform and then the door.
My hand trembled as I tried to engage the key with an equally rusty lock. The wind howled, the sea lashed against the breakwater, and the sky a purple haze of moving clouds in shades of light and dark. In hindsight, I should have brought someone with me, but who would have understood? Only Freddie and of course Theo and Phoebe would be aware of how I feel but they are not here. Anyway somehow I felt I needed to do this alone. At the same time, as I managed to unlock the door, I gave a hefty push and in I fell.
It was all there as I remembered. The two deckchairs, their colourful fabric once a bright cascade of candy striped colour now faded and worn. The smell of salt water long since dried to a powdery carpet on the floor. Rotting timbers which were once two sets of bunk beds lovingly created by Charlie.

The pretty china cups my mother always insisted we drank from. Red roses and blue forget-me-nots decorated the fragile saucers. A teapot, with a lid that didn't match but somehow fitted. A wooden tray now spotted with mildew was at one time adorned with a pretty marquetry floral pattern. I didn't really understand why Carrie hadn't taken these home. I knew she and Charlie had taken some things, but I presumed it was their way of not breaking ties with this shack completely, thinking they would be back to spend time here. A few more items reminiscent of my childhood. A metal bucket and wooden spade, a larger bucket for collecting driftwood, shells, seaweed, or anything else we could find. The kettle had almost rusted away. There was no sign of our two-ring Calor gas burner on which we boiled water for our tea and what Carrie called a swill down, translated as a wash, or the saucepans we used to make soup. This was an all-year-round seaside retreat, so soup was a must on cold blustery autumn/winter days.

I stood and thought, 'Is this it? Is this all that remains of my childhood?' My heart hammered in my chest. I felt tears fall down my cheeks. I fell to the ground and sobbed until there were no tears left.

I took what I wanted from the shack. The memories were all in my head, so nothing would ever replace those. I didn't bother to lock the door. What was the point? No one would be interested in anything I had left behind. Well, the shack was never really ours, and besides which we would not be using it again. Maybe someone else would take it on? Who knows! If they do, they will never know the joy or the fun we had or Albert whom we all missed very much. His hut still stood but only just.

I looked around at the greyness of the day, a slight drizzle mingling with my tears. I had one more job to do: it was their wish to have their ashes scattered here.

'Goodbye, *Mum* and *Dad*. Thank you so much for everything . . .' I thought I heard Carrie's voice whisper on the wind, 'You always had to have the last word, Jack.'

INDEX

A

Albert   5-7, 18, 28-9, 34, 36-8, 43-5, 58-9, 62-3, 71-2, 77-84, 87, 89-93, 95-6, 100-2, 104, 106-7, 109, 115
Amelia 'Milly'   53-60, 63, 66, 68-87, 89, 91, 94, 96, 102-7, 110-12, 114, 120
Anne   62-3
Anstruther, Arthur   81

C

Catrina   108, 112
Connaught, Carole   15-16, 25-6, 29, 31, 43, 49
Connaught, Caroline 'Carrie'   ix, 1-10, 12-13, 15-18, 22, 24, 26, 31-2, 38, 40-4, 47-50, 53-5, 57, 59, 61-2, 64-9, 71-3, 76-8, 81-3, 85-9, 91, 94-8, 100-1, 103, 105-6, 109-11, 113-15, 119-20
Connaught, John   15-16, 43

D

Drayton   100-1, 107
Drayton Electronics   100, 108

F

Freddie   4-8, 63, 71, 75-7, 89-90, 94-6, 109, 114

G

governors   40, 96, 98

H

home schooling   49, 62
home tutoring   15, 33

J

Jacqueline   62-3
Jarman, Derek   8, 93
Jones, Charlie 'Charles'   1-6, 9-17, 19-32, 34-47, 49-58, 62, 64-75, 78-9, 81-3, 85-7, 89-91, 93-7, 101, 103-15, 119-20
Jones, Jack   1, 7-9, 17, 42-7, 49, 51-2, 54-5, 57-9, 61, 63, 65, 73, 75-80, 82-91, 94-8, 100-10, 113, 115, 119-20
Jones, Phoebe 'Phebes'   1-2, 4, 9-10, 14, 17-18, 30-2, 34-9, 41-5, 47, 50-2, 54-5, 57, 61-5, 72-3, 75, 83-6, 88, 94-5, 97-8, 101-3, 106, 108-10, 113-14, 119
Jones, Theodore 'Theo'   1-2, 4-5, 9-10, 13-14, 17-18, 24-39, 41-63, 65-87, 89-91, 94, 96-8, 102-8, 110-14, 119-20
Joseph   5

M

Mark   112
Marriot, Felicity   57, 67-71, 74, 80-2, 120
Marriot, Nigel   67-71, 80-2, 84, 120
Mary   22, 25, 39-41, 46, 59, 88, 98, 106, 110
Morgan, Miller   40, 87-8, 98

117

P

Pat 3, 30-1, 38, 42, 44-7, 51-2, 54, 56-7, 63, 72, 75-6, 84, 86, 91, 101-2, 108, 112

R

Radcliffe Infirmary 50

S

Sheila 22, 25, 29, 39-41, 55, 59-60, 87-8, 98, 110
Stan 37-8
Stephen 61, 64-5, 72, 75-6, 83, 85-6, 88, 97, 102-3, 106, 109-10

T

Tale of Two Cities, A (Dickens) 35, 77
Tiger's Eyes, *see* Jones, Theodore 'Theo'
Transem, Maude 11, 13-16, 43, 51, 65
trustees 40-1, 99, 110

V

Vera 56

W

Walker 23, 30
Wellington 22, 24, 27, 30, 41-2

AUTHOR'S NOTES

Not many of us are fortunate enough to live the lives we choose. Compromise is normally the order of the day. However, I think Carrie and Charlie came close to their dream life. They were happy with what they had, which given their three successful children was quite a lot. It also came with hard work and dedication.

If Carrie hadn't met Charlie, who knows what she might have gone on to achieve. Having said that, I don't think he held her back. She was lost in a wilderness of loneliness and with no job or money. She met him just at the right time. Charlie had a quiet way about him reflected in Theo's personality. Carrie and Charlie loved each other dearly, and somehow they both wanted the same things, a stable family life and some adventure which time in the shack afforded them.

Charlie also had definite ideas and a little stubbornness born out in Phoebe who resembled him the most. He fell in love with Carrie the minute he saw her. There was no question he would have pursued her until she agreed to stay with him.

Jack somehow managed to be a chip off the block which formed his family. He was closest to Carrie and Charlie and hadn't quite got the determination needed to succeed in the way Theo and Phoebe did. However, that didn't deter him. He knew that whatever he chose to do would be okay with his parents, and because of that, he did extremely well in the end.

They all loved Albert who was stoical and stubborn. He knew little of the world beyond his environment, but somehow was happy and enjoyed having our family around.

When Milly's parents came on the scene, absolutely harmless individuals, the product of their background and altogether far removed from the day-to-day living of the Connaught/Jones family, Carrie and Charlie held their heads high and had every reason to. Nigel obviously did good works to receive his knighthood, but I think he would have probably come from a titled family anyway. Felicity just took up the slack so to speak. Milly didn't have an altogether unhappy childhood, just ignored mainly through her parents' hedonistic lifestyle.

As we know, the shack was never theirs, but they managed to hold on to it until they were too old and infirm to visit anymore.

Jack was always going to be there for his parents.

I could have taken this story on further but felt if I hadn't brought it to a close now, it could maybe have gone on for ever. So I decided to leave the Connaught/Jones family in peace! 'Thank goodness for that!' Did I hear you say, Theo?!

All of my characters are a combination of people I have met at some time in my life. But to avoid being sued, nobody in particular fits all the criteria!

There is a fair amount of poetic licence in this story; however, isn't that what fiction is all about?

Jeanette Voyzey.

Printed in Great Britain
by Amazon